SECRET
of the Second Door

Other books by Robert Colby

Fiction

Beautiful but Bad

Executive Wife

The California Crime Book

The Captain Must Die

The Faster She Runs

Make Mine Vengeance

Murder Times Five

Run for the Money

The Star Trap

These Lonely, These Dead

SECRET
of the Second Door
ROBERT COLBY

WILDSIDE PRESS
Berkeley Heights, New Jersey

First Wildside Press edition: September 2000

Secret of the Second Door
A publication of
Wildside Press
P.O. Box 45
Gillette, NJ 07933-0045
www.wildsidepress.com

SECOND EDITION

*To Marcia
and for
Tom and Diane Johnston*

Chapter One

*T*he clipping came to Shepard in the mail one day in early June. The envelope, typewritten and postmarked New York, bore the address of a place he had not lived in for years. The address had been crossed out and another written in ink. This too had been scratched — out and the Florida address, his present one, scrawled in pencil.

There was nothing in the envelope but the clipping.

Hotel Man Dies in Crash

Paul Kirby, 34, night manager of the Briteway Hotel near Times Square, was killed instantly late last night when his car overturned on Saw Mill River Parkway. State Police reported that Kirby was apparently intoxicated and driving at high speed. He failed to negotiate a turn, crashed into an island of the parkway, caromed off one tree, struck another, and overturned. Kirby was alone and driving toward New York.

The circumstances surrounding the accident mystified authorities when it was learned from Mrs. Corinne Kirby, wife of the victim, that Kirby had been missing since Friday night. Mrs. Kirby, 29, a striking redhead who lives at the Westbridge Manor on Riverside Drive, explained that her husband had quit his hotel duties early on Friday night but had not returned home. She said she had no knowledge of his whereabouts from Friday night until news of the crash reached her just before midnight Saturday. The situation was further shrouded in mystery when police discovered a .45 caliber automatic in a pocket of the dead man's clothing. Mrs. Kirby was at a loss to understand why her husband would be carrying a loaded pistol or where he got the weapon. An investigation is underway.

Neil Shepard read the item through rapidly the first time with increasing astonishment. He read it a second and third time slowly, studying each line until the facts were clear and he was finally able to believe them.

There was nothing in the clipping to indicate when this had happened, and it seemed important to Shepard that he know. The paper showed little sign of age and had taken less than ten days to reach him. Still, this proved nothing. It might have been mailed a long time after, though that seemed unlikely.

He turned the column over to a partial account of the opening investigation of a well-known labor leader for the misappropriation of union funds. The investigation had been given wide publicity and Shepard remembered it well. It had started three weeks ago.

With a sense of satisfaction, Shepard folded the item and carefully tucked it in a compartment of his wallet. The satisfaction came from knowing that Kirby had been dead less than a month. This would mean that Corinne — whom the reporter's glib understatement had called merely a striking redhead — would be still too mournful over her loss to have become involved with one of the male vultures who must be, even now, hovering near.

Or would she be mournful at all? Admittedly, Shepard didn't know. It had been nearly six years since he had had any real knowledge of her. And now he was a little surprised, a little shocked, to find that he cared.

How quickly we forget abuses. How easily violent passions are restored. They need only the small opening of a door long closed.

Shepard finished going through the rest of the mail automatically, without interest — mostly bills. He did something then he hadn't done for years. Though it was only ten minutes after eleven in the morning, he went to the liquor cabinet, took down a bottle of good bourbon, and poured himself a double shot. His hand trembled slightly and a few drops spilled on his shoe before he could get the glass to his lips. He squeezed his eyes shut and swallowed all of it as though it were some necessary medicine. He wiped his shoe with a cloth and went to the expanse of picture window in the living room. The window was round — shaped like an immense porthole.

He looked down from two stories upon the graying, rain-spattered face of the ocean. It had rained a lot that June along the Gold Coast of Florida, while the few tourists there during the intermission between the winter stampede and the summer flurry wept. And the natives, as they laughingly called themselves, applauded, liking the change from the endless glare of sunny days.

Neil Shepard lit a cigarette and exhaled with a long sigh. The tension was leaving him. It was ridiculous to conceal from himself his relief that Paul Kirby was dead — or more accurately — relief that Corinne was free. For he had not known Kirby, a man who had never been more to him than a name in a clipping, the first clipping having come in the same strange way, announcing the marriage. Though now that Corinne was free, he had no idea, what, if anything, he was going to do about it.

Shepard was a tall man and large. At thirty-two he had a look of bigness and robust muscularity. He had a full head of dark blonde hair, and his features were round and boyish, except for the hard thrust of jaw. His wide, pleasant mouth smiled easily, a helpful asset in the tourist trade. Few people noticed that while he was smiling his eyes were sometimes sad, sometimes cold.

The first clipping had come to him at the end of the Korean hostilities, as he was about to embark for home. At college, he had been a member of the ROTC, and this had brought him the dubious pleasure of being sent to Korea as an infantry lieutenant. What had ever made him think that a walking, magnetic mine of a girl like Corinne would sit bovine and docile, waiting for his return?

The newspaper item announcing her marriage — marriage, not engagement to that stranger, Paul Kirby, came as a double shock. He had received a warm letter from Corinne only the week before. And further, the Korean mess was over and soon he would be sailing for home, busting with his stupid plans for a hasty wedding and eternal honeymoon.

Nothing from Corinne — just the clipping — cold, anonymous, the address typewritten. It must have come from some jealous, frustrated female wanting to knife him for his neglect of her — some evil dame he had long forgotten. The hell with her. It didn't matter.

He had written Corinne a six-page letter. He knew it was only an outlet for his emotions — a useless crying in the wind. He tore it up. Then for years after, when she came unbidden to mind, he lied to himself that he didn't even care enough any more to hate her.

That sturdy old ambition for a stodgy but secure job had gone out of him. He had moved around a bit and he had done a number of things, some of them crazy and foreign, for excitement. He had been a dealer in Vegas, a bartender in New Orleans, a longshoreman in San Francisco, a charter-boat captain's helper in Miami.

He had made good money, too. More than he would have made at any routine desk job. And everywhere he went, he lived simply and saved. He didn't know why he saved — except that he was looking for an easy out — a way to make money and have time to live.

He found a way out along the Gold Coast of Florida. He bought a lonely, undeveloped piece of coast property below Pompano Beach. Quite a lot of cheap land. Pure speculation.

As he expected, in a couple of years the land in that section began to be bought up for the tourist traps — hotels, motels; nightclubs, apartments. The value of his property went up. He sold half of it, and with the money built a six-unit beach apartment house on the remaining half. He lived in one apartment and rented the others. He might never be wealthy, but with luck he would never have to do what he called real work.

The subtropical living was lush. While most of the nation huddled in the mean rooms of decaying cities to escape snow, slush and the cold of cracked and littered streets, he swam in the clear, luke-warm green of the Florida ocean and drank rum coolers beneath tall palms leaning in a tropic breeze. He listened to a few gripes, salved the little wounds of the tourists, and collected the rents. Simple. Magnificently easy.

Of course there were drawbacks. Taxes were high; there was upkeep and a fair-sized mortgage to be paid off. Thus his net profit provided only a decent living. What he needed was more capital. If he had fifty — even forty — thousand he could add units so that he would have more than just a living. But that kind of money was impossible to save. He would have to find some angle that had so far escaped him — maybe another piece of property bought low and sold high. Meanwhile, he had a very good thing.

He had, in fact, thought it would be the cure-all of his troubles. In the matter of work and finance, it was — but somehow intangibly it was not. He had found that you exchanged one kind of boredom for another. Low work was a bore — and so was no work. Gray skies and bitter cold were a bore — and so were sunny skies and languid heat. Dark buildings were a bore — and so were clean white ones, if you saw enough of them. Scrubby streets were a bore — and in time, so were sandy beaches.

So really, he didn't win after all.

Shepard poured another drink from the bottle. He sat down in a big chair next to the window and sipped slowly. He glanced at the phone on the table at his elbow, downed the drink, and picked up the receiver.

When the operator got the number through New York information, he told her to place the call station-to-station. He clenched the phone against his ear tightly, listening.

"Hello."

He kept listening.

"Hello. Is anyone there?"

Her voice was startlingly familiar. He opened his mouth to speak. He found nothing to say — not even hello. Quietly he cradled the receiver.

It was enough — she was there. He smiled. His eyes were at once sad and cold.

After a moment he heaved out of his chair and went into the bedroom.

Indiscriminately, and with frantic haste, he began to toss clothing into a suitcase.

Chapter Two

The Westbridge Manor Apartments were located in that area of upper Riverside Drive close by Columbia University. The building took up one entire corner and stood thirteen stories tall. Tenants on all but the lowest floors had a fine view of the park just across the drive, the river beyond with all its traffic, and the Palisades on the Jersey side. The long clean swing of the Washington Bridge farther uptown could be seen obliquely.

It was night in Manhattan — twenty minutes after nine by Neil Shepard's watch as he entered the lobby of the Westbridge. There had been a delay in getting him on a flight out of Miami, and after arriving in New York he had spent time looking for an uptown hotel. Then for a while he sat in his room, just staring at his unopened suitcase on the rack at the foot of the bed, the phone on the night table, the gray-streaked window, his shoes, the brass doorknob.

The first surge of impulse had left him, and he now felt a deep loneliness. He was astonished that he had taken the step at all and undecided as to what kind of reception he was going to have. And he wondered if he was a fool to humiliate himself.

Was it worth it?

*O*n another night in June six years ago, Shepard and Corinne had been dancing on the Astor Roof. They had just come from a Broadway musical — a light, frothy thing, held together more by the good music and comedy bits than by the thin love story.

Shepard and Corinne had held hands as they watched and listened from the twelfth row center of the orchestra. Shepard felt the mood of the songs, and, from the pressure of her hand, he thought that Corinne did also. Shepard knew that he had fallen in love in the way the songs told him love should be but rarely is. This love was so precious he wanted to guard it jealously. If it were possible, he would shave chained this thing he had in a vault of concrete and steel, to hold it there forever. But he knew this was not possible — or even desirable. And again, he believed as the songs told him — that at any moment the dream might vaporize and vanish in despair.

Yet he did not dwell on this. It ran like a theme in the background of his consciousness. On the surface he told himself that for him it was different. As death would come for others, so also for them would come the end of love's rapture. But never for Shepard.

The play had closed with a sweeping climax of the title song, the performers bowed, the curtain descended. The lights went on and for a moment they looked at each other and smiled, a slow moving of the lips and a meeting of the eyes. Her face was soft, she was supremely beautiful, and her smile communicated something for which there would never be an adequate word. Suddenly Shepard wanted to cry. So he turned away, stood, said brashly, "Come on, kiddo — let's go!"

They hurried along Broadway to the Astor and took the elevator to the roof.

Now the lights were soft, the music again wailed of

love, and they danced. Corinne was dressed in a white fluff of organdy with a splash of dark red flowers. She was beautiful, not only by Shepard's standards, but also in the eyes of nearly every man who covertly watched her.

There was a rhythm and harmony in the structure of her body. She was tall. She spiraled upward from round, slim legs — long tapered pedestals for the rich swell of thighs and arch mold of buttocks. Then the slender waist, a long sweetly narrow indentation before the quick thrust and high flare of breasts. Arms, shoulders, back were graceful. No harsh lines — everything flowed in curves. She stood straight and proud, yet easy, relaxed.

Her hair was long and of a deep burnished red. Her face was a soft U that widened and closed at the brow. She had a straight nose, and her eyes were large and green with amber flecks. Her mouth was wide, the upper lip long, the lower twisting downward to form a delicate sensual curve at center.

The face was intelligent. It was piquant, a little haughty — it knew she was all woman.

Shepard would have been better off if she were not so beautiful. The days of his reign would have been less uncertain. And his rapture, though not made of the same heady stuff, might have endured. But he didn't think about this, nor care. He was riding high on his wave of emotion. And only in startled moments of honesty would he admit that his hours with her might be numbered.

As they danced, Corinne moved closer to him, and he was conscious of her body and the excitement it stirred in him. He was not new to affairs with women but this was different. This was Corinne. He wanted to marry her. Trying not to be obvious, he removed himself a fraction from the close press of her limbs. That was better. Because now as he floated with her across the floor, the mood and sensation were ethereal.

She was so popular that Shepard had to hide his jealousy all the time. He did this very well. He knew that a beautiful woman was bored with too much attention and that short of an engagement or marriage, any attempt to withhold her from other men would mean the death of the love she had finally expressed for him. It was the old game. He hated it and loved it at the same time.

They had a final dance, and then it was tune for him to pay the check. The amount was large — this single evening would cost him about a third of his week's pay. At this period he was working for the photographic supply company where he had met Corinne when she had come to the office with a female photographer who wanted to make a purchase and register a complaint about an overcharge in billing. He was assistant to the office manager, and while the title was rather impressive the pay wasn't.

He was increasingly worried about money. But he hid this from Corinne, paying the check casually and leaving a handsome tip.

They drove in his car over the 59th Street Bridge to Long Island, where Corinne lived with a friend. Shepard put his arm around her, and she slid across the seat to be close to him. He snapped on the dashboard radio, and love music engulfed them in a quiet, pensive mood. They spoke little during the ride.

In front of Corinne's apartment building, Shepard parked the car and cut the motor. He lighted their cigarettes and, after a moment, he drew her to him and kissed her. They kissed again, this time for much longer. Shepard threw his fresh cigarette out the window, and she mashed hers in the ashtray.

She said then, "Don't you think it's awfully light here? If we're going to play it for the public, we ought to get paid.''

"Sorry," he said. "Thought maybe you might want to go in.''

"Not tonight, darling. No hurry. Tomorrow's Saturday, remember?'' There was a small note of sarcasm in her tone that he wondered about. Maybe she had been too careful in letting her know his interest was more than physical.

"Tomorrow should always be Saturday,'' he said. He gave her arm a squeeze, started the car, and drove around the corner. It was a side street and by an empty lot there were no lights. They slid down in the seat, he kissed her again. Thus far on his dates with her there had been a lot of necking, and once his hand couldn't help wandering to her breast. But when she had pushed it away gently, he had never tried again.

Tonight he sensed a change in her. As they kissed she turned sideways and strained against him. There was abandon in the movement of her mouth over his, and her breath came in short gasps of excitement. Instinctively he brought his hand to rest just under the firm hill of her breast.

Her hand rose to meet his, and, anticipating that she was displeased, he began to remove it. But now she had hold of his hand, astonishing him by pressing it palm inward at the place where the nipple was taut beneath her dress.

"I don't mind," she breathed, "not any more. Not with you, darling.''

He said nothing but obeyed as though it were a command. Some of the feeling of worship went out of him, and for a moment he just held his hand there idly while he adjusted to the change. Then he gave a mental shrug, his hand rotating, his fingers kneading. He knew the score. There was no hesitation about what to do. In less than a minute, he had fallen from his pink cloud into a whirlwind abyss of reality where there was another kind of love — perhaps more terribly binding.

But just once again he hesitated. This was when he was pushing down on the rim of her strapless gown and she was helping him at the second when she was free and he was staring in fascination at the white peaks of nakedness cresting in soft shadow. He still wanted to hold his conception. And he could do this if he spoke the only words he hadn't spoken. He pulled her against him so that now he couldn't see.

"Marry me," he said. "Oh God, Corinne, marry me! Every time I tell you I love you, that's what I mean. Will you marry me, Corinne? Will you?"

She went a little rigid in his arms. She drew back slightly and looked up at him. "Marry you?"

"Yes. Yes! Marry me."

She was silent. Then she said. "I — I don't know. I haven't thought about it. No, that isn't true. I've thought about it a lot. But I don't want to talk about it right now. Do you understand?"

"No. Not exactly. I mean —"

"Your thought is — it's — it's wonderful. But your timing is a little off, sweetheart. There are moods — Later. All right? For now, just make love to me."

His mind bent this way and that between gusts of desire and crosswinds of doubt. Again he adjusted, now giving in irrevocably to passion.

After a while she said, "I think we'd better stop."

"Oh God, honey," he answered. "Now you want me to stop. Now!"

"Love in the front seat of a car," she murmured. "Couldn't we go to your apartment?"

He didn't live far away, but he had never taken her there. He sighed and let down the last barrier. What difference did it make? Why not?

"Why not?" he said. "Let's go."

They drove along in silence. He was a little frightened of what might become of them now. But he needn't
have worried. When they left his place in the morning,
even in the bright glare of sun, he was, in a different
way, forever bound to her. And she had promised to
marry him.

And this was only one of many nights to follow. . . .

Sitting now in this hotel room years later, he remembered those nights in vivid detail. And understood
why he had to come back.

Chapter Three

*I*n the lobby of the Westbridge Manor, Neil Shepard
looked for the name above the brass mailboxes. He found
Paul Kirby, 7-A — the Paul scratched out and Corinne
written above it. Somehow the substitution of names told
him something about her. He stored it away for inspec-
tion and moved on to the elevator, wondering now if she
would be home at twenty minutes after nine in the
evening. But then, after all, it was Monday night. The
weekend was over.

He found 7-A in the front of the building — just a
door at the end of a corridor. He studied the door as
though it might whisper some small truth. He reached

for the bell and his hand dropped back again. His palms were moist, he was breathing deeply, his legs trembled. He stood very still. He turned his head slowly to see if the corridor was empty. It was. He leaned against the door and listened — nothing. Suddenly he stepped back and gave the bell a quick jab. Hearing the sound, he released air from his lungs in a long sigh. Some of the tension went out of him.

He heard movement behind the door. Then it opened.

She was so much the same he was unprepared, startled. Did he expect that six years would ravish her looks? Not Corinne. Her face was a little grave, there were shadows of fatigue beneath her eyes and she had gained a pound or two, maybe, but she was the same.

As before, the deep red hair spilled down from her head over her shoulders, every lock shining and in place. The contours of her face were soft and delicate, the skin pale and clear. The mouth was a red banner across her face, unfurling at the lower lip in a gentle pout of triumph. The head was held high and arched backward ever so slightly. The figure descended from proud hills to winding valleys of grace.

She stood there in a simple green sheath dress, on which there was embroidered a single cluster of spread-winged beige butterflies.

Only the dress was new to Shepard. She was the same.

They stood now like monuments to surprise, staring. She was the first to recover.

"Neil!" she cried, "Neil Shepard. I can't believe it! Come in. Come in!"

His eyes slid away from her face and down. He stepped quickly into the room as she closed the door. He looked up then, but not at her. He gave a quick, darting glance around him.

The living room was a large rectangle overlooking the river, the ceiling high in the manner of old buildings. The austere lines of the room had been broken by the furnishings — low, modern pieces rounding out corners, splashes of color breaking up the great stretches of empty wall. At a glance, the obviously expensive pieces seemed in good taste.

Shepard knew that she stood just behind him, waiting. Still he didn't speak. It was not a chasm of time that lay between them and kept him silent. Time vanished at the sight of her. It was more as if she had stepped into another room for a matter of minutes — perhaps only to change her dress. But while she was gone, he had looked into a dark closet and found the unbelievable evidence of her treachery.

Still, time was a factor in that it had softened his hate and bitterness — so much so that restored to her presence he had lost all desire to accuse her. For accusation, even when justified, debases the accuser still more than the accused. If it were possible, Shepard would have closed the door to that dark closet forever and gone on as before.

"Well," she was saying, "for heaven's sake, Neil — does the ghost speak? Does it tell why it has returned?"

"I live in Florida now, you know," he said without turning. "East Coast. Near Pompano. I own an apartment building on the beach. It does very well in the winter."

"Oh," she said with a little laugh. "That explains everything. Now I know exactly why you've come."

He swung around abruptly. Seeing her standing there was as confusing as staring unto the eye of a searchlight from the darkness. "Maybe I've come to destroy a memory," he said, "and take back a new one. Maybe that's why I've come."

Her smile held neither denial nor acceptance of

him. It was just a smile. "How simple you make it sound," she said. "At least you've told me one thing — I don't think you're married. Like a drink? Scotch or bourbon?"

"I haven't changed," he said.

"Bourbon and soda, then." She left the room in a symphonic movement of limbs.

He went to the window and looked down upon the ebony slice of river, the winking neon of the Jersey coast, the lace network of the George Washington Bridge — and, just below, the bright, fat bug of a bus scurrying uptown.

The ice-on-glass tinkle told him that she had returned.

"Beautiful view," he said. "Busy. Majestic. I look down on palms and sand. When you come by plane, the transition is fast — and interesting. It works both ways."

He went toward her a little stiffly. Their fingers touched when he took the drink from her hand. Their eyes held, his face solemn, her faint smile curious, charming. He dropped into a chair, and Corinne sank upon a vast, pillow-decked sofa, the long-stemmed crossing of her legs a whisper of sound.

Shepard raised his glass. "Old times," he said.

"And old faces," she replied.

"Change that old to familiar and I'll drink to it."

She laughed. "You look much nicer when you smile."

They drank.

She put down her glass and took a cigarette from a black china box on the coffee table, offering him one. He got them lighted with very little shaking of the hands and sat down again.

Corinne studied him. "I'll guess you've taken on about a pound a year," she said. "Six pounds. Technically, of course, it's five and a half years."

"Eight," he said. "Pounds, that is. You're right about the years.

"Otherwise," she continued, "you don't look much different. Except in the eyes. Mature? Grave?"

"Cynical," he said.

Immediately her face closed. She studied her cigarette, looked up. "I suppose it's absolutely necessary that we talk about it," she said. "I owe you that. But I can't tell you the truth. Not now. Maybe never. Do you want to hear lies?"

"No. When you get ready to tell me the truth, you tell me."

"Is that what you came for — to hear some sad, forgivable tale? And then have me get on my knees and say I'm sorry — is that it?"

He felt his anger rising. He choked it down. He puffed, exhaled, squinted at her through the swirl of smoke. "I don't know why I came. An impulse brought me. And a newspaper clipping."

"The one about Paul? I guess you'll want to know about that, too." She sighed, leaned her head back on the sofa, and closed her eyes, covering them with the long fingers of one dainty had.

"Did you love him?"

"Yes — at first. And then he changed. Not really, of course. It was just that I discovered more about him."

"Why?" he said. "Why did he disappear? And then get himself into such a drunken state he went off the road and killed himself?" Shepard wanted to know because the answer might explain — not Kirby — but Corinne.

The hand dropped down from her eyes, clutched the edge of the sofa until the knuckles were white. "I don't know. Not exactly." Her head came up, and her eyes sprang open — shining moist. "Maybe I drove him to it," she said.

He took a swallow of his drink. He didn't know what to answer. And then, against his will, he was saying, "It's possible."

"I never had much," she said, her voice soft, husky. "I had to wait on tables for part of the money to keep me in college. We were always poor. There was never enough of anything — not for fun, not for clothes, vacations, the smallest luxury. My father made seventy-two-fifty a week, clerking in a store."

"You never told me that."

"I had a lot more pride then. Anyway, I was starved for even a year of easy living. I had terribly expensive dreams and no one to pay for them. Paul had a trust fund settled on him by his father, who died long ago. The principal came due on his thirtieth birthday — while I was going with him. We were married three days later."

"You weren't going to tell me the truth," he said. "But I guess you have. You married him for his money."

"Partly. Also, I was in love with him then. Anyway, at the time I thought his fifty-thousand-dollar inheritance was about half the money in the world. It wasn't. He bought me a beautiful ring. And we had a big car — a Cadillac. A few thousand went for furniture. And clothes — lots and lots of clothes. And good times — the kind that cost money. Then he got a leave of absence and we took a trip to Europe — London, Paris, the Riviera, Rome, Switzerland — the whole beautiful continent. And when we got back we had about ten thousand dollars and a lot of unpaid bills. He never told me the money was going that way. He was so reckless and gay — gambling and spending as though it was going to go on forever. And I — I thought it would.

"Before the money went, he was going to buy a restaurant. Then have a whole string of them. Some crazy dream like that. It sounded good. I thought he would do it. He didn't really lie to me, but he blew it up until it was a kind of lie. I was furious. Because, really, all he had was that little night manager's job he got because his father used to own the hotel. The way we were living, it was nothing. I was after him all the time to do something big — go out and make some real money. He just laughed. He kept teasing me. So one time, in a burst of anger, I told him he was a flop, that I couldn't take it any more and I was going to leave him. I didn't really mean it. But it sobered him up, so I let him believe it for a while. And that was when the trouble started. That was when he began acting strangely — quiet, moody.''

"My God. Why didn't you tell him you weren't serious?''

"I was going to. But then one night he came home very late, a little drunk. He woke me up. He had an overnight bag with him. He opened it and dumped it on the bed. Do you know what was in it?''

"I can guess.''

"No, you can't. Never. It was full of money — stacks arid stacks. The bed was covered with it.''

"How much?''

She tapped her cigarette in an ashtray, fell back on the sofa, and closed her eyes again. "Two hundred,'' she said wearily. "Two hundred thousand dollars.''

"Two hundred thousand! Impossible. Where would he get that kind of money?''

She leaned forward tensely. Her eyes were wide with excitement. "At first he wouldn't explain it. He just dumped all those bills on the bed, and he said, 'You wanted money — there it is. Swim in it. Make a dress out of it. Light cigarettes with it. I don't care if you use it for Kleenex. It's all yours. But no questions asked. And no separation. You don't leave me. Never, understand?''

"And that's all he would say?''

"Yes — until I refused to touch the money unless

he told me where it came from.''

"Then what?"

"He said he won it gambling. In a poker game at the hotel."

"And you believed him?"

"Yes. Finally."

He shook his head. "That's too much to swallow. Two thousand, maybe. But not two hundred thousand."

"It wouldn't be so hard to swallow if you had known Paul," she said. "After I married him I found out he was an incurable gambler. The horses, dice, poker, anything. It was like a disease. If I hadn't curbed him, threatened, pleaded, he would have gambled away all our money before we could spend it. I watched him lose eighteen hundred at the dice tables in Vegas, thirty-one hundred at cards in Monte Carlo. I thought of the days when a hundred dollars was a magnificent sum to me — and I was furious. For a month I stopped being a wife to him in the way it hurt most. Any time he gambled I withdrew from him. And he quit. But it was always in his blood — and he was weak."

"Sure," said Shepard. "But two hundred thousand! Listen, you don't just fall into games where that kind of money is being blown. Not unless you're on the inside with the big spenders. Not unless you're another Nick the Greek. And if they did admit an outsider, he couldn't sit a hand without showing thousands."

"All right," she said. "That's about the way I looked at it. But Paul knew this game was going on night after night right there in the hotel. There were five men. He claimed he got to know one of them and was invited to join. Then he withdrew all of our savings. He took a chance on lasting long enough to win. And he did."

"Well, it's possible," said Shepard. "Anything's possible. And if he didn't get the money that way —"

"Then how else?" said Corinne.

"People, have been known to steal, embezzle"'

"I thought of that," she said. "I even mentioned it — half jokingly. And very seriously, Paul said, 'Do you think for one minute if I had stolen two hundred thousand dollars, if such a sum were missing, it wouldn't have made headlines? Every paper in the country would have carried something on it.'"

"He was right," said Shepard. "That makes sense." He was terribly curious about and interested in the picture he was getting of Corinne and Kirby. But he wished he could swing the conversation to the level of their own personal relationship, past and present. Watching Corinne, felt that everything she said had a consuming purpose, as yet unrevealed. "Yes," he said again, "it makes good sense."

"It does and it doesn't," she said. "There were flaws. I asked him who these men were. And he said he didn't really know — except they were big businessmen — very big. From out of town. So I told him to name one of them, any one of them. And he said that was silly, the names wouldn't mean anything to me. I kept goading him, and he kept dodging. Finally I said I thought he was lying. I challenged him to name one name — just one. 'All right,' he shouted, 'all right! Victor Sortino.' I asked him what this Sortino did for a living. Paul said he wasn't sure. But from the talk he had gathered he was a broker or speculator, something like that."

"I never heard of anyone by that name," said Shepard. "So anyway, what did you do with all that money?"

"At that time of night, we didn't know what to do with it. So we went down to the basement where each tenant has a storage compartment with a door and a lock. We hid the money in a steamer trunk under some old clothing. Paul said not to put it in the bank because we were going to move out to the West Coast and start over again. He was going to quit his job as soon as he could break in a new man. He hated that job anyway because it kept him working nights.''

"Well, I get the idea,'' said Shepard impatiently. "He won the money and he more or less redeemed himself in your eyes. So if everything was beautiful, why did he disappear?''

She lit a cigarette, got up and paced across the room, then came back to stand by his chair — so close there was a remembered scent about her, so close the urge to reach out and circle his arm about her was overpowering. But her face was intent, far removed from physical awareness of him.

"I can't tell you that,'' she said. "It doesn't matter now. And it's very personal.''

"But you know why he left you?'' Shepard asked.

"Yes.''

"And where he was going so fast when he was killed?''

"No.''

"And why he was carrying a loaded .45 in his pocket?''

"No,'' she answered. "Not that part either. And it frightens me.''

"I don't wonder,'' said Shepard. "There are some nasty implications. But at least you have the money. There's a lot of comfort in two hundred thousand dollars.''

She looked at him blankly. "No,'' she said. "That's just it. I don't have the money. Not a penny of it.''

Shepard paused in the lighting of his cigarette. "You don't have the money? Why?''

Her lips tightened. There was an angry set to her jaw. "Because when Paul disappeared that Friday night, he took the money with him.'' She sank back with a sigh. "And I've never been able to find it.''

Chapter Four

Shepard got his cigarette lighted and studied a moment. "You went down and looked in the steamer trunk and it was gone, I suppose."

"Yes. When he didn't come home Saturday morning, I decided he might have taken it. And he had."

"It wasn't with him in the car when they found him, obviously."

She shook her head. "The police turned over everything to me. At least I can only presume they did, not forgetting that occasionally there are dishonest cops. But if I rule that out — and I do — nothing. I even forced myself to go down and search through that dreadful, sickening wreck at the place where it had been towed in." She looked away. "But there wasn't anything there," she murmured. "I even looked around here. But I knew that was useless."

"I'm sorry," he said. "And maybe if I know more I can help."

"I've got to find that money," she said. "I've got to!"

"That was the biggest loss, wasn't it? The money. Not Kirby."

She bit her lip. "That's unfair. That's cruel!"

"Don't talk to me about fair play." The anger in him was rising out of the emptiness, the void of the past.

"Don't talk to me about cruelty. That's your department. That's where you shine. You're an expert!"

"Oh, Neil, Neil. It seems that way, yes. But that's
because you don't understand."

"I'm willing," he said. "My God, I'm too willing.
But I've been sitting here a long time and I haven't
heard anything that would help me understand."

"I know, I know. I've been avoiding an explanation
because there really isn't one that excuses me. Anything
I would say could only put me in a worse light."

"That's impossible," the snorted. "With my imagination, that's impossible. Why don't you try?"

"All right," she said firmly. "I'm going to say it once
quickly. And then you'll have to take me or leave me —
as I am now, not as I was then."

"Go on."

She puffed on her cigarette nervously, smoothed her
dress, shifted her position. "There are two parts to it.
One is intangible, in a sense, and the hardest to explain.
But the truth is that I was spoiled rotten by men from
the time I was sixteen — just because I was pretty.
There were few exceptions — not even you, Neil. At first
I loved the attention. It was exciting, terribly good for
the ego. And then, gradually, I became bored with it all.
After a while nothing becomes so dull as that which is
laid in your lap. So, by the time I met you, the only men
that really interested me were the ones I couldn't have."

She sighed, crushed out her cigarette, twisted her
fingers in her lap. "At first you seemed unattainable.
You said all the nice things but you stood off. You
weren't jealous, you didn't try to hold me in your own
corner until I couldn't breathe. You kissed me a lot and
that was about it. You didn't try to make love to me. In
fact, even when I wanted it, you seemed to resist it. That
ways terribly exciting and puzzling."

"I wasn't looking for that," he said. "Not exclusively. From you I wanted so much more.''

Corinne nodded. "I know. I know that now. But you must remember I was immature. Wanting what you can't have just because you can't have it is a sure sign of immaturity. Though, in your case, it went beyond that. I felt a closeness, a warmth and security — trust, too — that I had never felt before. But in some subtle way you changed. After that night that we — that we went to your apartment, the first time we made love —''

"Yes, and whose idea was that!" he snapped.

"Mine, of course. I take all the blame. But you did change. You began to ask sly questions about my dates. You were jealous. In your unobtrusive way you took possession of me completely. I was hemmed in.''

"My God, I was only human.''

"Of course," she said quickly. "But because of the way I was, that made me back off. When I promised to marry you I meant it. Yet, I still hadn't grown up enough to know what I wanted.

"Then, while you were gone, along came Paul. He was one of those men who had a talent for being completely casual with women. He would be attentive and flattering and still you could never tell if he really meant it. He was handsome. He was charming while he was with you, and at the sane time he didn't seem to care a hoot if he saw you tomorrow or next year. Even when he proposed to me, he had the air of one who is madly in love and yet will be perfectly self-contained if you turn him down. I know now it was a calculated effect. But it had the same power to intrigue. You could never have all of him, never quite get inside him.''

"So that was it," Shepard said brusquely, "I faded badly and you married him.''

"No, that wasn't all of it. Now comes the tangible part. He did have money, what seemed like an awful lot to me. I could always have men but I could never have enough money, never enough of the beautiful things and the good times money could buy. Paul seemed to offer all of that — and I thought I loved him, too. Oh, Neil, you never can know — unless you've been on the dreary edge of poverty all your life — what a terrible need it is to have the security of money and the pride and power that goes with it. And how could I know that Paul had money but no money sense, that he was a gambler, that he was weak and ineffectual, that the only way he could get fifty thousand dollars was to inherit it and then he couldn't even keep it. I lost my respect for him — and my love. It was an awful mistake. But I found out too late.''

"Do you think you've changed?" he said.

"I don't know. Of course I have in some ways. Intellectually I see a lot of things. But emotionally — I don't know. Certainly I've changed. Nobody stands still.''

"But you haven't changed your feeling about money.''

She smiled. "No. On the contrary. It's more necessary than ever. For my tastes, my dreams, I need a great deal of it. That's why —''

"Sure," he said. "Sure. That's why you want to find the two hundred thousand. Well, anyway, you've given me an explanation of sorts. It's better than wondering. Why didn't you write me how you felt? Why did you leave me hanging in space?''

"If you think about it," she said. "If you think about it carefully, you'll see that you could never put anything like this in a letter. It would be less cruel, less harsh to say nothing.''

"Nothing? You could at least have sent me the bare fact — 'I'm getting married.'''

"Oh, but I did," she said. "Who did you think sent you the clipping?''

"You!"

"Yes. If seemed the most direct, the cleanest way to break it. No phony, useless words of regret back and forth. And, Neil, I sent both clippings. The last one, too. Because I figured if you wanted to see me that would be enough and —"

"You bitch!" he said. "You cold-blooded, marble-hearted bitch. I ought to kill you!"

He meant it. He could feel the impulse crowding into his fingers as he began to push up from his chair.

But she was coming toward him. Her face had softened; her eyes were closed a little, demurely. And there was a familiar smile, the lips slightly parted and curved with shy invitation. It was the same smile she had given him on the night she had first come to his apartment — at the moment when they had gone into his bedroom at the instant before he had turned off the light.

"Don't be angry," she was saying now. "I'm lost and alone. And I need you."

"Oh, you bitch," he said. But she pushed him gently back into the chair and, easing into his lap, brought her ahead down — soft, sweet-scented hair spilling over his cheek, her lips barely touching his. "Hush," she said. "Hush, darling. Let it go. It doesn't matter. You're home now. I'll make it up to you. In an hour I'll mend a year. In six hours it'll all be forgotten."

An angry sound was rising in his throat. But her lips covered his and the sound died. Even the memory of anger was gone.

A short time later as he lay on the sofa, his head in her lap, she was saying, ". . . So you see, darling, you rushed to conclusions. I'm not all black. I handled it the way I thought best the easiest way for you."

"I'd like to see you handle it the hard way then," he said. But he was smiling. "You knew I'd come. You knew when I read that clipping I'd come, didn't you?"

She pressed her fingers gently at his temples. "I thought you might," she said. "I thought if you weren't married, you just might. But on the other hand, I didn't know your new address, and I didn't even know if the envelope would be forwarded to you."

"Well, it was," he said. "And that was either the luckiest break of my life or the worst. I suppose I'll find out which soon enough. And what did you really want of me? Everyone has his motives — especially you, Corinne."

"I had more than one motive," she said. "I was desperately lonely and insecure. I needed someone special. And I wanted to find out if there was still something between us."

"Well?"

"Oh, yes, lots of things. But I haven't sorted them out yet. It will take time."

"And what else did you want of me?"

She hesitated. "I'm only a woman," she said then, "and not too bright about the sort of complication Paul left me with. I wanted you to help me find the money."

"And then?"

"I don't know. I honestly don't. It depends. We might get a chance to spend it together. And then again we might not."

"You're so sure of yourself, kiddo," he said. "I might not want it that way."

"That's up to you — and me."

"All right, suppose it doesn't work out? Then what if I find your two hundred thousand bucks — thanks, Neil, old buddy, see you around?"

"We could make some kind of arrangement."

"You're damn right!" He sat up. "Next time I want

to come away smelling sweet whatever happens. So we'll settle it on a percentage basis — right now.''

"Say like ten percent — twenty thousand?''

"Say like twenty-five percent — fifty thousand.'' He was thinking of the units that could be added to the apartment house, the big, beautiful rents, the difference between a decent existence and plush living. But down inside he was soft for this woman — soft to the core.

"You've changed,'' she said. "You certainly have.''

"Maybe, maybe not. But I understand about money. I'd know how and where to use it.''

"All right, fifty thousand. I wouldn't know where to start alone anyway.''

"Why me?'' he said. "In the radius of a mile there are a thousand, ten thousand men who would beat the door down to take my place. Why me?''

"Because I trust you. I think you're the only man I've ever really trusted in my life. With you, I feel secure.''

"I'll have to swallow that for the time,'' he said. "Now, let's see what we've got and where we start. I don't like your holding something back from me about you and Kirby. I can't help you that way.''

"It's too personal for now,'' she said. "And it wouldn't solve anything. It would tell you why he left but not where he went or what he did with the money.''

Shepard considered. "From the newspaper clipping, he was headed toward New York when he was killed. That right?''

"Yes.''

"Did it ever occur to you that he was coming back here to you?''

"I thought of it, and it's quite possible. But I don't think he had the money with him. And he didn't leave it here.''

"Let's see,'' said Shepard. "The Saw Mill River

Parkway empties into Connecticut. Do you know anyone that way? Or did he?"

"No. And I don't have the remotest idea where he was going."

"How far from here on the Saw Mill was he when he was killed?"

"About twenty miles from the other end."

"Well, that doesn't tell us much — except that he probably was coming from some place in Connecticut. It's important. But we'll have to drop it for now. So, aside from that, we have nothing to go on but the name of one man. What did you call him — Victor somebody?"

"Victor Sortino. But that doesn't help us a bit."

"He was in the game, wasn't he?"

"Yes, but you're not trying to say he would know where the money is, are you?"

"Hell, no. But we have to start somewhere and I think we should start with him."

"Why?"

"Because," said Shepard, "I'll tell you one thing for damn sure. I don't want to get mixed up in this unless there was a game. And you don't either."

"You mean you think there might not have been a game at all — that he was making it up?"

"I didn't say that. And I don't want to believe it because I like money as much as you do. But you'll admit that his story is pretty fantastic and that there are a few holes in it. So I want to check it first. If we can find this Sortino maybe he'll talk. Because gambling, even in a private game, isn't exactly legal in this state."

"Isn't it wasting time, checking all that?"

"Maybe. But if that two hundred thousand isn't clean, you can waste a lot of time in the pen as an accessory."

"There's one thing that does bother me," said Corinne. "Why would a bunch of big businessmen use a seedy hotel like the Briteway when they could afford the Waldorf?''

"Well, of course they may have decided the Waldorf wasn't the safest place to hold a poker game with those stakes. But you have a point. I think the best thing to do first is to check the hotel register and see if there was a Sortino signed in on that date. From that we might also get his address. Do you know anyone over there who could get the information for you?"

"Yes, I think so."

He stood up. "Well, get it for me first thing in the morning. I'll see if I can run him down and ask some cagey questions."

"What are you going to do now?" she said, standing and clasping both hands together behind his neck.

"Right now, I'm going to my hotel and see if I can get some sleep, though I doubt it."

She pressed against him, kissed his cheek and crooned into his ear, "You don't have to go."

"I don't?"

"No."

Soft hands unbuttoned his coat and crept around to caress his back. Lips touched his ear-warm breath from a warm mouth. "You never used to send me home. Why should I send you away? I could love you again, darling. Not that baby-girl love, but the love of a woman. You do love me, don't you, Neil?"

Love. What is love? he thought. She was creeping over him like a warm bath. But for a moment he held the warmth away. "Do I love you?" he said. "I don't even know if I like you. But, yes. Oh, God Almighty, yes — I love you!"

"That's my baby," she crooned. She let her head rest against his and, draping a slender arm across his shoulders, began to walk him away, down a hall. Before the open doorway to a bedroom, she paused and smiled.

As one coming from a dream, Shepard returned her look and smiled back. But he felt a sadness he couldn't shake.

Eyes downcast, her fingers touched a button of her dress. Shepard watched the fingers, fascinated. Then Corinne stepped into the room.

He followed and shut the door behind him.

Chapter Five

*I*n the morning, Corinne put through a call to the Briteway and got the information. It was true. There had been a Victor Sortino registered on the night Kirby came home with the money. To Corinne, in her excitement, it seemed almost unnecessary to pursue it further. But to Shepard, there were still oddities.

There were three, not four men, registered with Sortino. Corinne had quoted Kirby as saying there were five men altogether. Of course, the fifth man need not have been registered. He might have been local and thus simply come to the hotel and joined the game. Still — and strangely, too — Sortino had given as his address the name of a New York apartment hotel — the Barrington — while the others listed themselves as out of Chicago. If Sortino had an apartment or even a room at the Barrington, why hadn't they played there? And if Sortino had a place to live, why did he stay at the Briteway?

Shepard was able to think of several quite logical answers. For instance, it was possible that these men had reason to feel that they would not be disturbed at the Briteway and so, over a period of days, used it as headquarters. But about the two hundred thousand dollars, Shepard did not want to guess.

Two hundred thousand. It had a smooth, lovely sound, the figures round and even. Too even. Shepard had asked Corinne a question about this: "Was the amount of the money exactly two hundred thousand? Not any more or any less?"

"Yes," she had said. "We counted it."

"What denomination were the bills?"

"All hundreds," she had answered.

Shepard was thoughtful. It was not entirely unreasonable to assume that they played with cash and that, in a large game, nothing but hundreds were used. But it was stretching the imagination to suppose that Kirby had won precisely two hundred thousand — not a cent more or less. It was possible, but a little unlikely. For one thing, Corinne reported that according to the bank Kirby had withdrawn nine thousand eight hundred and fifty dollars, closing his savings account. After depositing fifteen hundred dollars in a joint checking account, he must have gone to the game with the balance — eight thousand three hundred and fifty dollars. But he had come home with an even two hundred thousand. He had said nothing about having an additional sum in his possession.

Shepard asked Corinne questions but did not mention his speculation to her. Instead, he set out for the address given by Sortino on the register.

The Barrington Hotel Apartments on West 54th

Street was ancient. Shepard entered the lobby, a long, narrow affair of dim lights and stiff brocaded chairs. After the bright flare of morning sunlight, he had difficulty adjusting his eyes. In the gloom, he picked up his reflection in the mirrored doors of the elevators and saw the dark wood of the reception desk beyond.

As if to maintain the atmosphere, the clerk was dressed in navy blue, a white carnation in his lapel offering pale, though tired, relief. He was a small prissy man wearing octagonal nose glasses, and his hair was jet and sparse, a half dozen strands attempting to cover with a backward sweep the shine of his baldpate.

"Do for you, sir?" he said.

"I'm trying," replied Shepard, "to locate a Mr. Victor Sortino. Would you see if he's in?"

"Mr. Sortino was with us for a little over a year," said the clerk, "off and on. He was out of town weeks at a time. And then he was gone, vanished. No forwarding address. I try to impress our people with the importance of leaving some small clue as to where they're going. But then, you know —"

"Yes," said Shepard, "I know. But you have no idea as to how I could reach him? Some relative or friend?"

"If he had any relatives I was not aware of it," said the clerk. "And I never met his friends."

"He wasn't married?" said Shepard.

"Not to my knowledge."

"There were no belongings or furnishings he had to have sent to him?"

"No, sir. We have a few transients. But still, this is a residential hotel. All rooms and apartments are furnished. Mr. Sortino took his personal possessions with him. No one was even aware that he had left for good until one of the maids found his room completely barren of a single personal article. He was renting month to month. He vacated less than a week after he paid his last rent.''

"Is that so? How odd.''

"Yes, sir. Odd indeed.'' The clerk smiled confidentially. "Are you some sort of investigator? He never seemed like a man who would owe money.''

"No," said Shepard, "not at all. Just a very old friend. I've been — out of touch. Well, then, thank you. I'll have to find him by some other means.'' He turned away.

"Just a minute, sir,'' said the clerk.

Shepard returned. "Yes?''

"There just might be someone here who could help you.''

"Oh? Who would that be?''

"Ackerman. He's one of our boys — runs the elevator, does errands, carries baggage, that sort of thing.''

"He would know?''

"Well now, I can't say for sure that he would. He's switched to day man. Wife insisted because she was nervous alone. But at the time Mr. Sortino was a resident, Ackerman had the night duty. He used to run a lot of errands for Mr. Sortino. He might have some little clue for you.''

"Good,'' said Shepard. "Where will I find him?''

"He's up on the elevator now. Just ring.''

"Thanks for your trouble,'' said Shepard.

When the elevator came down, Shepard stepped on and said, "You Ackerman?''

"Yes, sir,'' said Ackerman, smiling. "For a number of years now. Quite a number.''

Ackerman was a very old, very beefy man with a great crest of white hair and pale gray, rheumy eyes. He stood with a slight lean, as though his feet had difficulty supporting him.

"We'll get along fine,'' said Shepard. "I like a man with a sense of humor. Could you use a five spot, Ackerman?''

"Depends on how far I have to go for it. Not much on walking any more.''

"All you have to do is stand right there and answer a few questions." Shepard removed a five from his wallet and twisted it around his finger. "Clerk tells me you knew Mr. Sortino. That right?"

Ackerman leaned against the elevator wall and shifted his weight. His big black shoes creaked. "Depends on what you mean by that," he said. "Mr. Sortino was a great card player. Played all night sometimes."

"How come he left in such a hurry?"

"Don't know. One night, real late, he come down with his bags and told me to take them to a taxi. Said he was goin' on a trip. Never come back."

"Any idea where he could be?"

"I might. Excuse me — but who are you, sir?"

"Just a friend. Lost touch with him. Haven't seen him in years."

"That's all right then," said Ackerman. "Didn't want to get on the wrong side of him. Heard him give the cabby an address on Sutton Place South, over to the East River. Easy to remember. Number Eighty. Real swanky section. Thought it was queer because he said he was goin' on a trip. Might be he was just stoppin' off there before goin' to the station."

"You're a big help, Ackerman. Have to find that old son of a gun. Hardly remember him. Wonder if he's changed. He treated you well and you liked him?"

"Sure. I like anyone who's free with his dough."

"Yeah. But did you *like* him? I mean, as a person. Speak freely, Ackerman. We're not really close friends. Business acquaintances, you might say."

Ackerman scratched his head and considered. "I didn't like him and I didn't not like him. Same way you feel about a statue — understand? It stands there and it looks at you and it don't do nothin' to you one way or the other. That man is carved out of ice and stone — no offense, sir.''

"You've got a good mind, Ackerman. That's Vic Sortino right down to his pedestal." Shepard passed over the five. "Thanks a lot, Ackerman. And keep it to yourself. I'll surprise him."

"I doubt it," said Ackerman. "But thanks for the fin. Good luck, sir."

Out on the street, Shepard flagged a cruising cab.

"Eighty Sutton Place South," he told the driver.

Chapter Six

*E*ighty Sutton Place South was quite different from the place Shepard had just left. It was a handsome building of yellow brick and glass, with clean, slender lines towering above the East River, terraced apartments, and a canopied entrance. The building couldn't have been over two years old.

A doorman in a light gray uniform touched his cap. Shepard nodded and moved on to the cubicle that contained the switchboard and its female operator, a trim, middle-aged woman with a pleasant face. It occurred to Shepard that, this being a weekday, Mr. Sortino must be presently engaged in whatever enterprise was his calling. He might also have been only a visitor to the building, not a tenant. Still, he might be known.

"Do you," he said to the operator, "have a Mr. Victor Sortino living here?"

Did he imagine it, or had the operator's welcoming smile weakened ever so slightly at the mention of the name?

"Yes, sir. He's in Mr. Kroger's apartment — fourteen-B."

"Kroger?"

"Yes, sir. Mr. Kroger owns the apartment. It's cooperative, you know. But Mr. Kroger's business takes him to Europe. He expects to be gone at least a year this time."

"I see. Well, I don't suppose Mr. Sortino would be in at this time of day?"

"Yes, sir," said the woman. "I believe he is. May I tell him who's calling?"

Shepard found himself a little off guard. He hadn't really expected to find the man at all, let alone at home. "My name is Shepard," he said. "Neil Shepard. Mr. Sortino doesn't know me or expect me. I was sent on an important matter by a mutual friend."

The operator looked dubious. "I wonder," she said. "Could you give me the name of the friend, Mr. Shepard?"

"Kirby. Paul Kirby."

The operator nodded, smiled, chewed on her lip. She plugged 14-B and flipped the key.

"Someone down here to see you, Mr. Sortino. A Mr. Shepard . . . yes, sir. He said you wouldn't know him, said a friend of yours sent him — a Mr. Paul Kirby. . . . You say you don't know a Mr. Kirby? Well, what shall I tell the gentleman? Would you like to speak to him? Yes, sir. I'm sorry. I'll put him on."

The operator looked annoyed, but she smiled at Shepard.

"Pick up the house phone over by that chair, please, sir. Mr. Sortino would like to speak to you."

Shepard sank into the chair and took up the receiver.

"Hello. Mr. Sortino?"

"Who are you and what do you want?" The voice was precise, without emotion or harshness. It was fathoms deep and flatly cold.

I'm King Farouk, you surly sonofabitch, thought Shepard. "I heard the operator give you my name, Mr. Sortino," he said.

"If I had recognized the name," said the voice, "I would have had you sent up."

"I explained," said Shepard, "that Paul Kirby sent me. He claimed to be a friend of yours."

"I don't remember a Paul Kirby. What's his business?"

"Right now that would be a tough one to answer, Mr. Sortino. He's been dead about a month. But he used to be in the hotel game. He was night manager of the Briteway Hotel. That mean anything to you?"

The silence was heavy with thought.

"Take the elevator to fourteen," said the voice. "Apartment B." There was a click. The line was empty.

*V*ictor Sortino opened the door. His attire looked expensive — shantung suit the color of okra, dark brown tie, white silk shirt. His grooming was meticulous.

He was a dark-skinned, dark-haired man in his late thirties, close to six feet tall. His shoulders were extraordinarily wide and slightly hunched over, giving him the look of some giant bird unfurling its wings for flight.

From a large chest cavity, his body fell away immediately to narrow waist and hips, long slim legs. It was a lean body, full of harsh but powerful angles.

His face was carved out of mountain rock, his cheekbones high and prominent, the flesh around them taut. The face below fell into deep hollows, then rose at the scoop of jaw. His mouth was wide and firm, his forehead a broad bony expanse. The eyes were ebony jewels, set in deep sockets. They were brilliant with cold intensity.

There was a remarkable stillness about the man — more a mental aura of waiting than a physical immobility.

Sortino managed to draw back his lips without smiling and with a slight twist of his head indicated that Shepard should come in.

It was a regal room, with mirrors in gilded frames, ornate pieces of French provincial style, dark woods, and rich fabrics.

Shepard followed Sortino's soundless footsteps across a beige carpet to a small study overlooking a flat swath of river.

Sortino designated a chair for Shepard and placed himself behind a large desk of dark walnut. His face empty of expression, he waited in disconcerting silence.

"You do remember Kirby, then?" said Shepard.

"Maybe. What are you selling and who are you?"

"I have nothing to sell and I'm a friend of Kirby's widow. He was killed in a car crash a few weeks ago. I came for some rather personal information."

"What information?" Sortino still hadn't moved in his chair.

"Before he was killed," said Shepard, "Kirby brought home a large sum of money. He told his wife he won it in a poker game. It was more money than mast people ever win in poker games so she wasn't inclined to believe him. However, he mentioned you as being present during the game and she asked me to check.''

Sortino picked up a letter-opener and twirled it slowly: ''Who are you?'' he said.

''I told you, my name is —''

''Shepard,'' finished Sortino and waved the information away with an impatient gesture. ''I know your name — what's your business?''

''There's no connection. I'm merely acting as a friend,'' said Shepard. ''But I operate an apartment house — tourist accommodations — in Florida.''

''Prove it,'' said Sortino. ''You must have business cards, a driver's license issued in the state of Florida.''

''Why should I prove anything?''

Sortino leaned forward suddenly. ''Look, Shepard. Do you think I'm a goddamn fool? Do you think I let just anyone in here off the streets to ask me questions? Come on, come on! Hurry it up, I'm busy.'' He sank back and waited.

Shepard had no choice. He contained his irritation and removed his Florida driver's license and a traveler's association card from his wallet. He dropped them on the desk.

Sortino studied them carefully, returned them without comment.

''I realize,'' said Shepard, ''that you might be reluctant to discuss anything as personal as a private poker game. But I understand about gambling. I used to be a dealer in Vegas. And I'm only interested in establishing for Mrs. Kirby that Paul Kirby was in a poker game and that he won a large sum of money. Just tell me that much and I won't take anymore of your time, Mr. Sortino.''

''How did you find me here?'' said Sortino.

''Briteway Hotel register.''

Mr. Sortino shook his head negatively. ''I gave the

Barrington, and they don't have a forwarding."

"I know," said Shepard. "I went there. I was lucky.
Boy who took your bags to the taxi heard you give this
address."

"You went to a lot of trouble," said Mr. Sortino.
"Too much."

"Sure, but did you know Kirby?"

"I forget names. I meet a lot of people. But it comes
back to me, yes. We called him Paul and he was night
manager, I guess — slim fella, pretty boy with a mus-
tache?"

Shepard recalled the eight-by-ten framed photo-
graph Corinne had shown him. "Yes," he said, "that's
Kirby."

Sortino's face remained inscrutable. But the skin
around the knuckle-thrust of cheekbones spasmed
tighter by some quick pulse of thought. "I remember
that one, all right," he said.

"Then he did join you and your friends at poker
there at the hotel?" said Shepard.

"He was at the desk," said Sortino, "when I stopped
by to pick up a telegram. I had a racing form in my hand
and we got to talking about the horses. One thing led to
another —"

"And so you invited him to join the game?"

"There's no harm in telling you now," said Sortino.
"It's past history and nothing could be proved. Yes, I
invited him. Too bad."

"Very costly," said Shepard. "He won a very large
amount, didn't he?"

"It depends on what you call large. You divide the
loss among a few wealthy businessmen and they'd never
miss it. But would you call five thousand a large
amount?"

"For me, yes. But it would be only a fraction of the
sum I had in mind."

"All right," said Sortino. "The play is over. You called me and I'll show two hundred thousand."

"Exactly!" said Shepard. "We understand each other. It won't go any further. Mr. Sortino. And you've done me a big favor. Just one more question. How did it happen to come to precisely two hundred thousand?"

Sortino swung his chair toward the window and back. "That's easy," he said. "After the game, there was a high-card draw and Kirby quit when he had the even two hundred."

"I see," said Shepard. "Good enough. Well, that's all then."

Sortino brushed an invisible speck from his trousers. And when he looked up, Shepard had the feeling that he was smiling, though he underwent not the least change of expression.

"Tell me," said Sortino. "As a point of curiosity, what did Kirby do with all that money?"

"I haven't the faintest idea," said Shepard honestly.

"Is that so? No idea at all, have you?"

"No."

"Well, it doesn't matter now. I suppose his widow will have plenty of use for it. Attractive girl, is she?"

"Beautiful. Proud as a rich man's yacht and just as graceful."

"And just as fast?"

"Shut up!" barked Shepard. "One more like that, Sortino, and — I'll climb over that desk."

Sortino remained poised and still. "I wouldn't try that," he said. "You might have a bad accident. Besides, I was just probing the relationship. You said you were friends. It's a very loose word." Again he seemed to be smiling. But his face was a blank.

"Sure, and you have a loose mouth, too," said Shepard. He had what he wanted and he was too enraged to care what he said now. "What do you do for a living, Sortino? Anything? Or is this a day off?"

If the man was angry, he didn't show it. "Whatever it is that I do," he said almost pleasantly, "if you'll get out, I'll be able to do it."

Shepard got up abruptly and found his way to the door. Sortino followed.

"I suppose I should say thanks," said Shepard.

"I've never needed them," said Sortino.

Shepard turned and left. All the way to the elevator, he felt the man's eyes on his back. There was something about Sortino that made him want to turn around suddenly and shout some obscenity.

But even as the thought came to him, Shepard heard the thin snap of a door closing — a stealthy sound in a quiet corridor.

Downstairs in the lobby, Shepard stopped at the cubicle and spoke to the operator. "I wonder," he said, "if you could give me Mr. Sortino's business address. He forgot to give me his card and I might want to get in touch with him at his office."

"I'm sorry, sir," said the woman. "I don't know his business address or even what his business is. But I could get him on the phone for you."

"Never mind, thanks. He's busy now and I won't disturb him. What did you say was the name of the man who's in Europe — the one who owns the apartment?"

"Kroger," she said. "Mr. Martin Kroger."

"Oh, yes, Kroger. Well, I imagine Mr. Sortino must be in business with him. What's his line?"

"Why, I believe it's a kind of loan company. Although Mr. Kroger would die if he heard anyone call it that." She smiled. "A very ritzy establishment, you know. It's the Mutual Security Exchange Company — over on Fifth Avenue."

Shepard thanked the woman and, frowning, went

out to the street. Walking slowly west, he tried to decide if there was really any point now in making a call at the Mutual Security Exchange Company.

Chapter Seven

Victor Sortino closed the door thoughtfully when he saw that the man called Shepard had reached the elevator. Eor a moment he rested the broad arch of his back against the door and slowly, absently, removed a slender cigarette case of monogrammed silver from his breast pocket. He tapped a cigarette against the case with a precise, mechanical movement, flipping it over and repeating the process with the other end. He put the cigarette between his lips unlighted and held it there a moment. Then he reached for it, glanced at it, and crushed it between thumb and forefinger.

Now he moved without haste across the room and re-entered the study. He dropped the broken cigarette from his palm to a wastebasket, brushing his hands together to remove a few fragments of tobacco. He slid behind the desk, sank into the wing-backed chair, and took from a drawer the weighty volume of the Manhattan phone book. He flipped the pages, then paused, running his finger down a column until he came to Kirby, Paul.

He pulled a pad toward him and, with his desk pen carefully copied the address and phone, number. He folded the paper and tucked it in his wallet.

Now Sortino pushed out of his chair, slid back the panels of a wall cubbyhole beneath a bookcase, and removed a bottle of Scotch and a glass. He poured a small amount, inspected the amber liquid, then went to the kitchen where he added ice and soda. He returned and stared at the phone. Again he sought the Manhattan book and thumbed through it. Picking up the receiver, he dialed a number.

"Briteway Hotel," the, girl answered.

"Let me speak with one of your employees — Mr. Paul Kirby," said Sortino crisply.

"I beg your pardon — what was that name, sir?"

"Kirby. Paul Kirby."

"I'm sorry, sir. Mr. Kirby is no longer with us."

"I see. Well, it's not important. I'm from out of town and someone asked me to look him up. He was one of the room clerks, wasn't he?"

"No, sir. He was an assistant manager. Night manager, you might say."

"Uh-huh. No idea where I can reach him, have you?"

Silence. Then — "I'm afraid he died, sir. I'm sorry. Perhaps someone else could help you."

"No. It had nothing to do with accommodations. But thank you."

Sortino hung up. The room was beginning to smolder with midday heat. Sortino closed the windows, and the distant scattered sounds of the city that rose in muted peaks faded, leaving a vacuum in which he could hear his own breathing. He closed the door to the study and switched on the window air-conditioner, the hum and whirl of it accompanying his thoughts as he tapped another cigarette on his case, this time lighting it.

For a long time, Sortino stood rooted before the window. As he remembered the details of a night in which there had been vast treachery and tortured death, sifting the known facts and balancing them with conjecture against the unknown, only the hand with the cigarette moved from mouth to side and back again.

The cigarette had long been replaced by another, and that one too had burned away when suddenly he made a great fist and drove it into his palm with finality. He turned, sat down on the corner of the desk, and again took the receiver from the phone. If there was one thing about which Sortino prided himself, it was his honesty. He was going to share the news. And, in the end, the original split would go through. He dialed.

"Hello — Jake?"

"Yeah. That you, Vic?"

"Who does it sound like? Now, listen to me. The lid has blown off the Briteway deal. — We were crossed, but it wasn't Kroger."

"Jesus, God! You sure?"

"If I wasn't sure, would I say so?"

"Christ! What a hell of a thing."

"Never mind. It's too late to weep now. And I'm not going to explain on the phone. But there's a chance we can pull a squeeze and recover. You understand what I'm saying?"

"Sure. I get it."

"Then get hold of Max and Goldy. All of you hop down here for a conference and a little finger exercise this afternoon. Be here at four o'clock sharp. Bring the car. And, Jake — don't miss. This thing is hot!"

"Right, Vic. I'll pass it. Four o'clock, sure."

Sortino set down the receiver. His face was perfectly blank. Nevertheless, he felt as though he were smiling broadly.

Chapter Eight

*I*n the swelling blister of noonday heat, Shepard walked west until he located a drug store. Once inside, he found a booth just vacated and ordered a sandwich and milk. In the cool of air-conditioning, the flush of heat left him and he was better able to think.

He was still undecided. Sensibly, he should not explore the thing further. Sortino had admitted that Kirby won the money in a gambling game. He had even explained how the amount happened to be precisely two hundred thousand, how he had met Kirby, and how Kirby managed to worm his way into the game. There were other questions he might have asked Sortino — How many were in the game? Who were they? And what was their business? Why did they allow a stranger to draw cards in a game of such high stakes unless they intended to take him? Instead, they lost to the one outsider.

The truth of it was that if Sortino had a legitimate business, it was probably remote and secondary. If ever there was a man who looked the part of the professional gambler, Sortino was he. Undoubtedly he and the circle in which he moved were super-gamblers, bookmakers, even syndicate operators of secret, illegal gaming rooms in the private precincts of gaudy-faced nightclubs. So what? Am I, thought Shepard, a one-man clean-up-vice campaign? Let it go. The police have their ways. And their numbers. He was no puritan. He had as much use for dollars won gambling as those won in the sweat of work.

But in the end, a deep intuition of trouble and an inescapable logic won him over. The trouble was only a gnawing, indefinable uneasiness inside him. But on top of all the other little loose ends of untidy facts, logic made him wonder at the astonishing picture of men like Sortino and his breed allowing a weak and vulnerable amateur like Kirby to walk away unchallenged with two hundred thousand dollars of their money. Legitimate businessmen, yes. Wealthy playboys, yes. But in the cold, black depths of Sortino's eyes, he had seen no businessman or playboy; no resignation to sportsmanship or the tired shrug of the good loser.

There was, in the whole affair, the stink of something beneath the surface that needed digging up and airing before he was going to let himself or Corinne look for two hundred thousand dollars' worth of trouble.

The money, if it had remained hidden this long, wasn't going to vanish in the hour or two it would take him to stop by the Mutual Security Exchange Company and the Briteway Hotel. There was nothing to lose but time — of which, at this month of the year, he had an abundance.

And in the front of his mind was the persistent hope that, in tracing the by-paths that wound back to Kirby and Sortino, he might possibly come across a clue that would lead to the hiding-place of the money. Practically, he could think of no better approach.

Shepard paid his check and headed for the row of phone booths and the city directory.

*T*he Mutual Security Exchange Company was housed on the third floor of one of the clean-faced regal buildings that touch Fifth Avenue and comprise that cluster of towers bordering Rockefeller Center.

Just inside there was a semi-circle of bleached mahogany desk, behind which sat a youthful blond girl in a quiet costume and manner to match. Beyond her, through a wide doorway, Shepard could see a long, glass counter displaying watches and gems, and a row of offices containing closed, numbered doors. From the center, behind partitions, came the busy clack of typewriters.

"I came," said Shepard, "to see Mr. Martin Kroger."

"I'm sorry, sir," said the receptionist, "but Mr. Kroger is out of town. In Europe. And I can't tell you when he'll be back. Is there someone else who could help you?"

"Who would be in charge in his absence?"

"Miss Buckley. She's our general manager. I imagine she's about to leave for lunch, but I'm sure she'd have a minute. Would you like me to send in your name?"

"I don't have a card, but the name is Shepard — Neil Shepard. Just tell her it's a personal matter concerning Mr. Kroger."

"Certainly, Sir. Just have a seat."

Shepard sank into a heavy red leather chair and waited. The girl picked up one of the phones on her desk, buzzed, and spoke briefly, nodding. He was unable to hear what she said.

"Miss Buckley will see you, sir. Straight ahead as far as you can go, then turn right."

Shepard approached the office and peered inside. He didn't know what he expected to find — Perhaps a rather shrewd, though prim, middle-aged spinster.

He was surprised.

Though not beautiful, the woman behind the ample desk was certainly attractive — and young. Not much past her mid-twenties, she had tar-black hair, medium short and cut in bangs across her forehead. Her eyes were a deep quiet blue; her face had a delicate, almost elfin quality of alertness. It was a face that should have been frivolous and instead seemed rather grave in repose, a little sad.

When she stood, as she did now, she was slightly below middle height, small-boned with a pert little figure that blossomed unexpectedly at the bosom.

Now she smiled, and the smile was quite charming.

"This is it, Mr. Shepard," she said. "Come right in."

Shepard entered, closing the door behind him. The office was small, neat, and cheerful, with discreet touches of color. It was a room more intimate than imposing.

Miss Buckley extended her hand across the desk and, after Shepard had taken it, indicated a chair. She met his gaze with a bright expectancy. "What can we do, for you, sir?" she asked.

Shepard had already decided that he was in luck. Miss Louise Buckley was a person who looked both warmly human and perceptive. Talk with her should be easy and relaxed. Still, it was difficult to begin.

"Actually," he said, "there was a personal matter which I wanted to discuss with Mr. Kroger. But now I find that he's in Europe."

"It's not unusual," said Miss Buckley, offering him a cigarette from a case on her desk and lighting one herself. "Mr. Kroger is often in Europe, sometimes on buying trips, sometimes on problems connected with our offices in London and Paris. We're a small company, but a busy one. I'm afraid that most of the time I'm left to handle things here. So if there is anything of a business nature —''

"No," said Shepard. "But, thanks anyway. Purely personal. Do you know when Mr. Kroger will be back?''

A slight frown crossed her face. Her smile was apologetic. "Normally," she said, "I would have a pretty good idea. But in this case — I just don't know. He left very suddenly to cover some emergency about which I'm still in the dark. The fact is, I haven't heard from him recently. So, you see, I just couldn't tell you when he'll return. I'm sorry.''

"That's all right," said Shepard. "I suppose it will have to wait. By the way, since it was a personal matter, I went first to see Mr. Kroger at his apartment on Sutton Place. I was a little surprised to find someone else living there, a rather — what shall I say — uncommunicative and strange fellow by the name of Sortino — Victor Sortino.''

There, he thought. I'll just drop that one in her lap and see what she does with it.

Her face became grave — the same expression he had caught in the moment before she looked up to see him standing in the doorway.

"I only met Mr. Sortino once," she said carefully, "when I stopped by to locate some papers which Mr. Kroger had taken home with him to study. They were papers that had to be signed and returned to me before he left. In his haste, he must have forgotten." She swiveled away, then back again. "Mr. Sortino is rather different," she said cautiously, "but he was most helpful.'' She seemed about to go on. Instead, she merely dragged on her cigarette and looked at him in her soft way.

Discretion, thought Shepard. She knows when to stop.

"Well," said Shepard blandly, "I thought since he

was living there, he might be a partner or a member of the firm. I thought he might be able to help me — even on a personal matter. But he didn't say anything about Mr. Kroger, and he wasn't very cooperative.''

"As far as I know," said Miss Buckley, "Mr. Sortino has no connection whatever with the business. Obviously, though, he must be a good friend of Mr. Kroger's since Mr. Kroger left word that it was all right for him to use the apartment in his absence. Whenever he's going to be gone for long periods, he permits friends to use his apartment. It would be a shame to let such a beautiful pace go to waste.''

"Yes," said Shepard, "wouldn't it? Then Mr. Kroger told you personally Sortino was going to take over his place?''

Miss Buckley began for the first time to look at him with a somewhat puzzled, if not annoyed, expression. From this, he gathered that while her attitude was not necessarily secretive, he had asked too many questions.

After a moment's hesitation, she said, "Mr. Kroger did mention Mr. Sortino to me on the phone." She leaned back and now her expression seemed to close the subject.

Shepard pulled in sail and steered the conversation in another direction. "Tell me something about your operations here," he said. "I'm more the pawn-broker type and I'm not up on loans for the Four Hundred. In fact, I didn't know they needed them.''

Miss Buckley laughed frankly and musically, and the tension that had been building in her eyes disappeared. "Well," she said, "we don't exactly cater to the Four Hundred. But somewhere between the pawnshop level of borrowers and the upper crust, there are some people in the pretty high-income brackets who, for one reason or another, get into temporary financial trouble. But while these people are temporarily out of funds, they are usually well supplied with valuable jewelry and other articles that are highly salable and make good security. It's these people that we help — and, of course, in turn help ourselves." She fiddled with her bangs. "You'd be surprised at the high-grade people who need money in a hurry — until payday — even for a weekend. I could tell you some very funny and some very sad cases."

"I imagine," said Shepard.

"Of course, we also sell mounted diamonds and other stones, some of them unredeemed, others purchased by Mr. Kroger in Europe or elsewhere."

"Interesting business," said Shepard. "And if you'll excuse my saying so, you seem very young for the responsibility of taking charge — even in Mr. Kroger's absence."

"Oh, I have a lot of very qualified help," she said.

"The people who evaluate behind those numbered doors."

"Yes. And then I grew up with the business. I was Mr. Kroger's secretary fresh from business school. And he grew to trust me." She smiled. "Wisely, I hope."

"I don't think he made a mistake."

"Thank you."

"What's he like — Mr. Kroger?"

Her face clouded. "I thought you knew him.'"

"On the contrary. I was hoping to meet him for the first time."

"I see." She nodded. "Well, in this business we might say that he's an uncut diamond."

"Naturally, you wouldn't say diamond-in-the-rough any more than you would say — hock shop," said Shepard chuckling.

"Exactly." A smile hovered on her face.

Well, thought Shepard, the warm-up is over. Guess I'll have to make ready for the dive.

"I can't help getting back to this Sortino," he said.

"He's such an odd duck that I'm curious about him. Have you ever heard Mr. Kroger speak of him at any length before? Do you know anything about him at all?"

Again Miss Buckley's face closed — this time more suddenly, more positively. "No," she said. "I don't know the first thing about him and he was never, except in passing, the subject of any conversation I had with Mr. Kroger. And now, if there's nothing else, I hope you'll excuse me because I was about to go to lunch."

"I haven't offended you?"

"It's not that at all," said Louise Buckley without the least edge of irritation in her voice. "But for anyone short of a detective, you do ask a lot of personal questions. And if you are one, I wish you'd make it known."

"Would it make any difference?"

"Of course. Then we could talk more openly about whatever is bothering you."

"Is there anything bothering you, Miss Buckley?"

"Why do you ask?"

"Because I think there is."

"I'd have to know more about you before I could answer that."

"Well, I'm not a detective, private or otherwise. But I might as well be because I'm playing the part. I don't even live in this state. I came up here from Florida only yesterday to help a friend of mine whose husband was killed in an automobile accident. Maybe that isn't why I came in the first place. But it turned out that way. So it amounts to the same thing. Actually, my business is rentals — seasonal — for the tourists on the east coast of Florida. I own an apartment house."

For a few minutes he unfolded the picture of himself and Corinne, leaving out personal, intimate details. He felt that he could trust Louise Buckley, that she knew very little of whatever was going on and that he really had no choice in trusting her, within limits. He had to start somewhere, trusting someone.

"You might say," he finished, "that Corinne sent for me. Because she needed help in finding out certain things about her husband's affairs." He paused because he didn't quite know how to take it from there.

"You're having trouble telling me," she said sympathetically, "aren't you?"

"Yes. I guess I am."

"Well, talk around the things you don't want to discuss. Just give me the general idea."

"That's a large order," he said. "Because to make you really understand, I'd have to be terribly specific. But the idea, as you call it, is this — I'm trying to track down a sum of money which Kirby hid before he died and which has never been found. The money once belonged to Sortino and his associates. You could say they turned it over to him in payment of a debt. In some ways I don't understand why they paid Kirby the money in the first place, and I know nothing of what he did with it. Nor does Corinne, his wife. His widow. So I thought Sortino might throw some light on the subject and I went to him. You see?"

She smiled a rather sad little smile. "I see and I don't. What had this to do with Mr. Kroger?"

"Truthfully, nothing. But when I pried so little out of Sortino, I got to wondering about the relationship between him and Kroger. I thought through Kroger's office I could find out more about Sortino. Because somehow I think he has answers he hasn't given me. And if I could understand him, even what his business is, I could understand why he's holding back."

"You didn't find out Mr. Sortino's business?"

"No. Did you?"

She shook her head. "I haven't the vaguest idea. You came to the wrong place. Of course, if he would, Mr. Kroger could tell you."

"All right," said Shepard, "I've opened up as much as I can at the moment. So now you tell me what bothers you about Victor Sortino."

"How did you know that he bothers me at all?"

"Every time I mentioned his name, your face sent me messages."

"I must wear a better mask." She lighted another cigarette from the stub in the ashtray and her hand shook slightly. "The fact is," she said, "I really have nothing very tangible against Mr. Sortino. But he does bother me. Perhaps I'm just allergic to his type. He's been perfectly polite and all that. It's just that, well, in a quiet sort of way he makes me uneasy. I suppose it's because he has one of those terribly cold, walled-in personalities with about one-tenth of what he is or thinks showing. I've never liked the type and he's about the best example of it I've ever seen. You feel that inside he must be like a bomb ticking away. Because no one could be that contained without exploding sooner or later."

"That's a very thoughtful study of Mr. Sortino," Shepard said. "Anything else?"

She chewed her lip. "A couple of little things. I can't quite picture Mr. Sortino and Mr. Kroger as friends. Not so friendly that Mr. Kroger would invite him to live at his apartment — even while he's gone. Of course, in his own way Mr. Kroger is something of a mystery to me, too. He's out of the office more than he's in. And much of the time I have no idea where he goes, why and with whom. It's almost as if the business weren't terribly important to him. But I've met some of his friends and most of his business contacts, and Mr. Sortino doesn't seem to fit. Normally, if someone were going to stay at his place, Mr. Kroger would explain who that person was. Because I have a key and I might have some reason to go over there while he's out of town."

"But in this case he didn't explain?"

"No. He never mentioned it. Except on the phone from the airport as an after-thought. He brushed right over it."

"He phoned from the airport?"

"Yes. He flew to Europe. Paris. But oddly, he never mentioned to me that he was going before he made that call. He sounded terribly strained, upset, hurried. I could hardly understand him. He wasn't on the line a minute — just told me to take care of everything, there was an emergency and he didn't know when he'd be back. Then he added that Mr. Victor Sortino would take over his apartment, treat him right if I saw him. Then he just hung up."

"Well, I suppose he made it all clear in a letter when he got there, didn't he?"

"No. He didn't. And if you want to know what's really bothering me, that's it. He's been gone about a month and I haven't heard from him by letter, phone, or cable. Nothing. He usually phones or writes within three days after he arrives. But, no. Nothing. And he knows there are all kinds of loose ends for him to take care of."

"Did you try to contact him?"

"Yes. Of course. They've heard nothing from him in either the Paris or the London office. They didn't even know he was coming."

She looked at him steadily. "You know," she said, "this is the first time I've really talked it out. But I'm worried. I'm terribly worried."

"You're a very nice person to have such a burden alone," he said — and meant it. "I'd be willing to share it with you over lunch. I've had mine, but if you have no plans, I'll buy yours and have a double Martini. I could use it."

"I have no plans," she said. "And I might want to

drink my lunch, too. So thanks, I'll take you up. I'd be grateful to have someone to talk to."

She got her purse from a drawer and stepped from behind the desk. "You came in to tell me your troubles and ended by listening to mine," she said at the door. "It's not very fair."

"Possibly our troubles are connected," he said.

"Possibly," she answered. "Some, but not all of them. Looking at you I find other things."

"What things?"

"Never mind," she said, opening the door.

But he caught her arm. "No, tell me," he said. "What things?"

She turned back. "You have the loneliest eyes I've ever seen."

"Me!"

"I'm sorry." She smiled her sad little smile. "I shouldn't have said that. Come on. Let's go to lunch."

Chapter Nine

Earlier, about the time Shepard was leaving the building on Sutton Place, the phone was ringing in Corinne's apartment on Riverside Drive.

"Hello."

"Hi, baby."

"Lloyd?"

"I was in the neighborhood and I had the hunger. So I called."

"What kind of hunger?"

She could almost hear him smiling, but he said only, "To see you, of course."

"Guess you'll just have to go hungry, Lloyd. I can't see you. I really don't want to. It's over. I told you that."

"Yeah, you told me. But you didn't mean it. Just your conscience talking. Listen, hon, don't blame yourself. He was a dope — a weakling. It would have happened anyway."

"I wish I could believe that. But I can't. If he hadn't come home and found us here —"

"Now look, baby, don't. Especially not on the phone. If I could come up and talk to you for just a few minutes, I think I could convince you you're whipping yourself for nothing."

"How? You don't know any more than I do."

"You're wrong. I have some ideas."

"What ideas?"

"You think I'm going to discuss it on the phone?"

There was a silence in which her thoughts raced around possibilities.

"All right. But ten minutes. No longer. Where are you?"

"Couple of blocks away."

"The male ego. Such confidence."

"Who should be more confident? I'll be right over."

Corinne hung up and went out to the kitchen to mix a batch of Martinis. She felt disturbed, and a drink might help. But this was a mistake. She resisted Lloyd about as effectively as she would an advancing steamroller. Ten minutes would stretch into an hour. And though Shepard said he had a lot of ground to cover and would be gone all day, giving her a call before he came uptown, it was taking a chance. And she needed Shepard. Almost as much as the money, the financial security, she needed the emotional security he gave her. There was a certainty, a predictableness about the constancy and magnitude of his love that gave her strength and ease of spirit. Since Paul's death, her guilt made her feel debased. And though Shepard saw some, not all of her weaknesses and unintentional cruelties, he didn't really believe them, didn't watt to. He whitewashed her. And in doing so, he helped her to uplift her own conception of herself. He filled some of the void of her guilt. But not all — not nearly all. So now perhaps Lloyd had some fact, even new rationalization that would let her escape entirely from her conscience.

Lloyd Gannon was sales manager for one of the big tire companies. He took two- and three-hour lunches with the top executives of vast empires, always paying the tab himself — off the expense account, of course. And before the cigar smoke had cleared, deals were made, contracts promised. Soon, whole fleets of trucks riding on rubber bearing the trademark of his company would roll down the highway — all because Lloyd Gannon had lunch with the right people. Or so he said. And likely it was true. He had the gall to sell snowshoes in Hawaii.

Lloyd was thirty-eight. He was tall. For Corinne, all men were tall. He had reddish-brown wavy hair, bushy brows over sharp gray-green eyes, a cleft chin, and heavy mouth. He was good-looking in a defiant sort of way. For Corinne, all men were good-looking, one way or another.

He was recently divorced from his second wife. Corinne had met him at the same cocktail party where she met Paul Kirby. But at the time, Lloyd had been married and she didn't allow herself to become interested. Long afterward, when Paul's money had drained away and most of her ardor had gone with the knowledge of his unchanging weaknesses, she ran across Lloyd at Schrafft's on Fifth Avenue. His wife was in Reno, and now he seemed fascinating with his breezy successful executive manner, his invincible ego, and his casual approach to even the most beautiful of women — Corinne Kirby. So they stole a few evenings together while Paul performed his managerial tasks at the Briteway.

Unfortunately, Paul was in the habit of calling several times during the evening — "So you won't be lonely, sweetie, and you'll know I'm thinking about you." Thus it was necessary for Lloyd and Corinne to spend a good deal of their time together at the Riverside apartment. Necessary, but never dull.

And then on that Friday night, the night after Paul had brought home the money, she had again been with Lloyd at the Riverside apartment for what she told him — and believed — was the last time. It had begun with her firm explanation that she and Paul had come to an agreement and were moving to the West Coast. That was the way it began. But it ended behind the locked door of her bedroom. It was an unpremeditated concession to Lloyd and to herself. A physical concession. Another finality.

Lloyd was air inescapable force. She did not trust him. She did not even like him. At times, she hated him. He brought out the worst in her — the evil, the animal side of her inclinations. His maleness, his ego was more than a match for her. It overpowered her. Every time she had him, it was as though she tried, in a frenzy of passion, to drain him of his smug power and take that power for her own. So that in their lovemaking there was nothing of love and tenderness, but only debauchery. So that when he was absent she hated him. And when he was present she had to have him. And the cycle wouldn't stop.

But it did stop. It stopped when they came out of the bedroom late that Friday night and found Paul's cigarette lighter on the coffee table and his hat on the couch. He had taken both with him to the hotel. And so they knew he had come home early and moving quietly, listening, had, found them out. And then he must have sat there nervously smoking — his mashed cigarette was in the clean tray — trying to decide what to do while they were oblivious behind the door of the bedroom.

And he must have come to some decision, some wild but perhaps unfinished plan. For he had left in a hurry — without the hat and the cigarette lighter.

She had phoned the hotel and had learned that Paul had turned his duties over to an assistant he was already breaking in for his job, and that he had left early. As she put down the phone she was then absolutely certain — and so despised herself — that when Lloyd came near, she struck him across the face and told him never to come back.

When Paul did not return the next day, she went down to the basement and found the money gone. Then, late that night, came the news of his death in the accident. Lloyd had called when he saw the item in the paper, but she had refused to see him.

She had never thought of trusting Lloyd with the secret of the two hundred thousand dollars. But she had been hovering dubiously around the thought of hiring a detective when Shepard at last came on the scene.

Shepard the eternal giver, she the endless taker. Poor Shepard. Well, he would have his reward. Maybe she would marry him. Yes, maybe she would. If she could find that kind of love for anyone again she might marry him. Even so, that might be the worst thing she could do to him. She was perhaps incurably spoiled and she would, sooner or later, need the attention of more than one man. And then she might destroy Shepard as she had Paul.

She didn't know. She was terribly confused. She couldn't think of anything else now but the money. Paul had carried no life insurance and there was only a few hundred dollars in the bank separating her from some awful drudge of a job. And she wasn't going to marry under the pressure of money while two hundred thousand dollars was just sitting somewhere rotting, doing no one an ounce of good! If she could get it, then she could think — think —

The bell rang. She set down her Martini and opened the door. Lloyd came in wearing a rich gray gabardine and his charming world-is-my-oyster smile.

"You look good," he said. "My God, that's the understatement of the year. Are you real?" He gave her a pat on the rump. "Yep. It's real. Cushion rubber, full tread, blowout-proof. Rides like silk but wears like iron."

She winced. Lloyd was insultingly earthy sometimes, but often a relief from the mooing adoration of more dependable males. He built no castles around her, and so she could be herself.

Lloyd gave the door a backward kick and, walking with his jaunty step, made for the sofa. He fell onto it with a sigh of possessive satisfaction. He never entered a room he didn't own immediately. Grand Central Station belonged to him if he were there.

"I made Martinis," said Corinne.

"So I see. Just a dash of olive in mine."

Unsmiling, she poured from a shaker, set the drinks on the coffee table, and sat down beside him.

Lloyd sipped his Martini, raking her sideways with his eyes — a bold, lusty appraisal. He set the glass down and produced a cigar from a leather case in his breast pocket.

Corrine reached out suddenly and grabbed the cigar from his hand.

"What the hell!" he said.

"Please, Lloyd. Have you forgotten? I can't stand those things. They stink up the place for days."

"I haven't forgotten," he said, taking the cigar out of her hand with a twisted smile. "But I always thought it was because you didn't want the smoke to tell tales. Anyone around to care?"

"Does it make any difference? Now?"

"Hell, no. Why should I care if you tread water between times?"

"I never tread water," she said. "I might sink into a pool of boredom and never come up. But I think cigars are about as romantic as chewing tobacco."

"All right," said Lloyd, putting away the cigar. "You double-talked your way out of that one. Give me one of your sissy sticks."

She handed him a cigarette and lighted it for him. He puffed, took it out of his mouth, and studied it.

"Like holding a toothpick when you're used to a baseball bat," he said, chuckling. His hand wandered over the top edge of the sofa and came to rest on her shoulder. "When are we going to get back to normal? How long are you going to pretend to mourn the guy?"

"What is normal?" she said. "Sleeping together?"

He gave her a look. "I told you — any time you want to make it legal —"

"No thanks. It wouldn't last a week. Now, what did you have to tell me? Or was that one of your sales talks? Because if it was, don't even bother to finish your drink. I told you I didn't want to see you again."

"The trouble with you is that you don't really know what you do want." He smiled. "But I do."

"Shut up! Just shut up, Lloyd. Or get out." But she

knew he was right. His very presence in the room was magnetic. Against her will she could feel the force of his magnetism.

"All right," he said. "I did get to thinking about Paul and that night, and it didn't make sense to me. I think you're knocking yourself out for nothing. You're blaming yourself because he got drunk and ran off the road and killed himself. I want to hear your reasoning again. First you tell me what you think happened. Then I'll tell you where you're wrong."

"You know very well what I think. He came home early and we didn't hear him because the bedroom's down the hall. He probably thought I was asleep and he walked up to the door to come, in. Then he heard voices and he listened and, of course, he knew right away. But he didn't know what he was going to do. He may even have tried the door and found it locked.

"So then, he came out here to the living room and he sat on this couch and lighted a cigarette. He must have put it right out because it was hardly smoked. He was terribly excited and nervous. So much so that when he got some crazy idea, he hurried off, leaving his hat and lighter. He went over to the garage where we kept the car and he drove out of town on the Saw Mill — God only knows where. He probably stayed at a hotel over-night and all the next day, trying to decide what to do. Saturday night he got drunk and started for New York. I don't know why. But he was in a hurry. He may have been coming back to talk it out and maybe forgive me, rushing because he knew I was worried. Or, more likely, he was coming back with that gun to kill me. Or you. Or both of us."

"Okay," said. Lloyd. "That's one story. And I don't believe it. Why did he come home early? For conversa-tion? — Or living it up? Both of those he could have any time, so I doubt it. Why would he leave a new man on

the job for that — a guy who didn't know the ropes yet?
No. I think he had some other reason to come home early
— some emergency — something he found out he had
to do in a hurry. He had to get something — and go
somewhere. I don't know where the hell he had to go.
But what he had to get was the gun — from a closet or
a drawer — some secret place he had hidden it.

"We'll never know why he had to get the gun.
Maybe he was in some jam — maybe he was afraid. Why
does anyone get a gun? Either they're afraid or they want
to kill or rob someone. Since he didn't rob or kill, he was
afraid. He was running somewhere, from someone. And
what he had to get that night before he left, was the gun.

"All right. So you don't know he has the gun and he
doesn't want you to know. Or what he's up to. Far from
going to wake you, he's trying to be quiet. He comes in,
drops his hat on the sofa, lights a cigarette, puts it right
out, leaving the lighter on the table. He's excited and he
forgets the hat and lighter. All he wants is the gun. It's
in one of these rooms, but not the bedroom. He doesn't
hear a thing. He gets the gun and dashes out as quietly
as he came. What, happens after that is anyone's guess
— except that he got loaded for other reasons and
crashed. And get this bit of logic — since he had the gun,
if he had known I was with you in that bedroom, he
would have kicked the door in and used it! End of story."

Corinne nodded. She kept nodding her agreement,
full of relief. "Yes," she said. "Oh, dear God, I think
you're right, Lloyd. It sounds so completely logical. And
I thought the whole thing — his running off, the drinking, the crash, even the gun, was because —"

"You see?" he said. "You see? You were way off
base. The guy was in some mess of his own making, and
he didn't know about us at all." His arm tightened
around her shoulder.

It was perfectly, beautifully true, she thought. Especially knowing what Lloyd didn't — that Paul must have had some reason to want to hide the money. He had come back to get it and the gun to protect it. Of course, if you followed that line of reasoning you could wonder about a lot of — other things such as why he should have to hide the money and protect it or himself in the first place. But she didn't want to think about that right now. In her sudden release from guilt, at least the guilt of having indirectly caused Paul's death, she was too happy.

She sighed, sank back, and gave Lloyd a bright smile of relief.

He took it as a signal. Immediately his hand slid down over her shoulder and cupped her breast. He turned against her and clamped his lips hard over hers, his other hand busy along her thigh.

At first, she sat perfectly rigid and allowed him to paw her. She felt unprepared. There was a small barrier in her mind. Very small and very thin. It came down slowly as she began to feel her skirt being lifted and disappeared altogether when his hand crept upward over her bare leg, paused tentatively and went on and on.

She sighed against his lips. The tension, the fear, and the self-accusation went out of her. All thought drained from her mind and there was only a willowy void of sensation to which she gave herself entirely.

Then he was standing and leading her by the hand to the bedroom. At the door her eyes looked frankly into his and she gave him a bold look of challenging sensuality. He answered with a pleased smirk and a sly wink. They passed inside.

She wanted to tease him. She went to a chair and sat down primly, arranging her skirt.

"What the hell," he said. "You want to blow the lid off?"

He came over and stood behind her chair, reaching down to fumble with the buttons of her jacket. She sat there with her cat smile until he had finished. She let him fumble with the bra until he was cursing, then she helped him.

Now she stood up, tall and proud, her shoulders back, hair dancing as she began to move across the room, her high taut breasts barely nodding with her stride. She looked at herself in the mirror, one hand on her hip, the other following the upward curve of her breasts until it covered the pink rigid bursting of her nipples. Suddenly she pivoted.

"How do you like me, darling?" she said.

"The way I spell *like,* it's *r-a-p-e,*" he said. "I swear to the devil — at this moment, I'd sell my lousy soul for you."

With a pretense of boredom, Corinne came and leaned close against him, studying her fingernails. "Lots of men have said that in other ways," she murmured. "Some have sold out completely."

"Yeah, and one ran away because it was so good he couldn't stand it."

"You shouldn't have said that," she came back sharply, pushing him off.

"Aw, I was just kidding." He went toward her and, sweeping her against him; began to kiss her neck and shoulder. "Oh, honey, baby, I'm mad about you. No more fooling. I can't take it." He looked meaningfully at the bed.

"No," she said. "I'm out of the mood now." She broke away from him and began to dress quickly. She was thinking that too much time had passed and Shepard might return with news he would forever keep to himself. The bed and Lloyd were available any time, but not the two-hundred thousand dollars.

"God damn it!" he said. "What's the matter with

you today? Please, hon. Don't be like that.''

"Don't be angry, darling. It's this place. Full of rotten memories. I freeze right up.''

"How about my place? It has no memories and no conscience.''

"When?''

"Tonight. Tonight!''

"I can't. Not tonight. My lawyer is coming over,'' she lied. "Something about Paul's will.'' She began to apply make-up, studying herself in the mirror.

"Aw, put it off. You can see him any time.''

Standing there so broad and intense, Lloyd looked like a seething volcano in which she would like to be consumed. There had been enough of gentleness the night before.

"I'll see,'' she said. "I'll see.''

"No, don't see, just do it!''

"Honestly, you're so demanding. Call me later and we'll talk about it.''

"What time?''

"Any time,'' she said, wanting now to get rid of him. "If I'm free, we'll arrange something.'' She finished with her make-up and gave him a fetching senile.

"That's my girl,'' he said. "That's my girl.''

She went with him to the door.

"On the cheek,'' she said when he bent over. "You'll wilt the tulips.''

He kissed her cheek. "Oh, hell,'' he said, grinning broadly, "it's just as well. I have a lot of work to do yet. And it would have finished me for the day. Call you later.''

As soon as she closed the door she began to scurry around, emptying the ashtray, taking the shaker and the glasses to the kitchen, washing them and putting them rapidly away.

She went back into the living room as the phone

began to ring. Shepard, she thought. Right on cue. She took up the receiver. But when she answered, no one was there. At least they said nothing and then clicked off.

She frowned as she hung up. It was a little scary when people got you on the phone and then wouldn't talk. If it was a wrong number, why didn't they say so? Rude. No consideration for anyone but themselves.

She picked up the morning newspaper and sat down. She couldn't concentrate. The whole world was simply leaping around at her pleasure. And yet, suddenly, she felt depressed and lonely and frightened.

She wished that whatever Shepard was doing, he would hurry back to her.

Chapter Ten

*I*n the end, over the third Martini, Shepard told Louise Buckley everything. She was so sympathetic and intelligent, so obviously guileless, that he felt he could trust her with Kirby's story of the money. Finally he gave her a quick picture of his relationship with Corinne.

"Now I begin to understand why you have such lonely eyes," she said.

"Why?"

"Well, you've been carrying that great big torch all

alone for years. . . . But then, you've found her again —
so why do you look so sad? You should be Happy Eyes,
not Lonely Eyes."

"It beats no eyes at all," he said. "And what do you
know about torches?"

"I had to learn the hard way." She smiled. "With
torches is there any other way?"

"Care to explain?"

"Not now. I've got to get back. Some other time,
maybe."

"If there is another time."

She looked at him solemnly. "Be very careful," she
said. "You could get way over your head in this thing."

"I'll be careful. By the way, what does Kroger look
like?"

"I won't try to describe him," she said. "But back
at the office I have a snap I took of him. For Christmas,
I got one of those Polaroid cameras with a flash attach-
ment, and I had to try it out on him in his office. He
wasn't at all pleased — but I got the picture."

Before he left her, she showed him the snapshot. He
had a vague, undeveloped hunch about Kroger and, on
the strength of it, took the photo along with him, promis-
ing to return it the following day.

Next Shepard made a stop at the office of one of the
tabloids. He spent a fruitless hour leafing through the
pages of newspapers that dated before and even after
the day of the accident that killed Paul Kirby. Kirby
himself had told Corinne quite logically that the theft of
two hundred thousand dollars would be headline news.
For that very reason, Shepard didn't expect to find anything. Further, he didn't believe the money was stolen,
but it seemed necessary to check out every possibility.
He couldn't forget the gun that Kirby had been carrying,
and, if the money was in any way connected with a crime,
there might be some hint, some indirect lead in the

papers.

But he found nothing. There were, of course, a number of thefts in all categories — with sixty-seven thousand stolen from a bank taking top honors. There were a dozen or more assorted murders. Shepard took special note of these — especially where the motive was robbery. But most of the murders were crimes of passion and, when money had been stolen, the amounts were comparatively small. The only other crime of any importance had taken place not before, but a week after Paul Kirby had showered Corinne's bed with greenbacks. It was a second-page item about the torture-murder of a man called Rick Trainor — no previous police record, no history of his activities. The man had been mutilated beyond recognition and the papers he carried had proved to be phony. Well, Shepard had found about what he expected — exactly nothing. Now there was only one more place to go.

*T*he Briteway Hotel was like any one of a dozen you can find on the side-streets off The Great White Way — a narrow entrance beneath a soot-dark marquee, a small lobby trying to look bright and busy and not quite making it, a single bank of elevators to rooms on the borderline between plain and grubby rooms full of anonymous shadows often more or less as borderline as their surroundings.

Shepard inspected the exterior of the Briteway, shrugged, and went inside.

"Kirby?" said the room clerk, a thin, pale young man who looked like there was little he hadn't seen, while remaining still unmoved. "Sure, I knew him. What about him?"

"How well did you know him?"

"Police?"

"No," said Shepard. "Just a friend of his wife's."

"Some looker, that one."

Shepard tightened his lips.

"What did you want to know about Kirby?" said the clerk. "I never saw him much except when I was going off shift."

"In that case," said Shepard, "I'd better talk to someone who knew him well. No use repeating myself."

"I could suggest several people," the clerk said. "Depends on what you want."

"I'd like to know if anything unusual occurred during one of his shifts."

"Little woman can't figure out why he took a powder — that it?"

"That's it."

"Well, neither can I, fella. And listen, as far as anything unusual happening during his shift — in this place that's every night in the week. You mean trouble with the guests, don't ya?"

"Something like that."

"Well, anything big, I woulda heard of it. But for that sort of thing there's always a security officer around. He and Kirby would have handled it together. Guy you want is Mike Connors, the night man. He comes on at four. You got about an hour to wait."

"I'll be sitting there by the newsstand," said Shepard. "When he checks in, would you ask him to come over?"

"Sure thing. I'll tell him."

"Thanks," said Shepard and, crossing the lobby to a faded pink divan, sat down.

For a while Shepard sat framing the questions he would ask the house detective — Mike Connors. Then he thought about Louise Buckley. She was great — deep, sensitive, loaded with character. She was also attractive, just the sort a sensible guy should find worthwhile. But there was no sense in love. There was only the wild excitement, the special need for one person. There was no such thing as a purely intelligent, unemotional choice. Corinne, baby — how will it end?

For Shepard, the lobby of the Briteway faded. In a dream he passed with Corinne into a bedroom and closed the door, remaining in the soft fold of her nakedness for a long time.

*E*xcuse me, sir. Did you ask for the house officer?"

Shepard looked up, startled. The house detective wore no derby. There was no soggy cigar clenched between his teeth. He was a medium-tall, fiftyish man with a mild, pleasant face, gray hair, gray suit, tolerant blue eyes. Shepard liked his looks and decided he was a guy you could talk to easily.

"You Connors?" he said.

"Yes, sir. Something I can do for you?"

"If you can spare me a few minutes, have a seat," said Shepard.

"I could spare an hour right now," said Connors, smiling and folding himself onto the divan. "A little later I might not have a minute. What's on your mind?"

"I'm Neil Shepard. Never knew Kirby, but I'm a good friend of his widow, Corinne."

"I only met her once," said the house officer. "But she's a very lovely little lady. Terrible thing, wasn't it? I'll never understand exactly what happened to Paul."

"Well, Corinne doesn't understand either. And that's why I'm here. She thought someone who worked closely with him might shed some light."

"I doubt if I can help you there," said the detective. "I liked Paul. But he was kind of a strange duck. Moody.

He was either way up in a balloon or down in the basement and couldn't find the light switch. When he was way up there, he talked like a man who had just left J.P. himself and was sure the deal would go through.''

"Big dreamer, huh?''

"Mister, they don't build bigger dreams than that lad could shake up. I used to kid him about it. I'd say, 'Paul, why don't you lend me that pipe sometime? Let someone else have a puff before you smoke yourself right out of this world.' Good guy, though. Easy-going. Used to wonder about him. Try to figure him out. Way I finally tabbed him was this — he was a guy who was forever lookin' through a telescope at some mountain he was gonna climb. Then when he found it was too high for him, his balloon would come down and he'd crawl into that basement. That was Paul.''

"I suppose he was in one of those basement moods that week before he died.''

"No, sir, not exactly. But he was worried.''

"You know it's no secret that Kirby was gambling practically all the time,'' said Shepard. "Corinne told me about it.''

"Well,'' said Connors, "it was pretty common knowledge around here. I'd say it was a disease with him. But I didn't know if his missus was aware of it.''

"Sure. It was the root of most of his trouble.''

"It figures,'' said Connors.

"Why?''

"He was in hock most of the time.''

"Cards?''

"No,'' said Connors. "The horses.''

"You never saw him play cards?''

"Not around here. But the bookies were in him for a wad.''

"How much would you say?''

Connors looked at him carefully. "I couldn't say for

sure. Placed his bets on the phone. But it ran into the thousands.''

"How do you know that?"

Connors lighted a cigarette and puffed. "Guess it wouldn't hurt anyone now. Told me he owed the book so much money you could buy a small house with it.''

"And did he pay?"

"Finally," Connors said. "He was trying to figure a way out. But he was scared to mess with those guys. Suicide. Asked my advice and I told him they'd get him sooner or later, police or no police. So he went down to the bank and drew out almost all his savings. It made him sick. But he paid.''

"When was that?"

"Couple of days before he ran off and got himself killed. Funny — because it looked like he welched and was on the run. But I saw him give a fistful to a runner the book must have sent around. Said he cleaned up what he owed. He wouldn't have lied to me about it.''

"And that was just a couple of days before he quit early and disappeared?"

"That's right," said Connors.

Well, thought Shepard, that blows up one part of his story. Kirby used the money he drew out of the bank to pay his tab with the bookies, not for a big card game. "Do you know who was making book for him?" he asked.

"No idea at all," said Connors. "Never saw anyone but that runner and didn't know him. With that kind of money it must have been a pretty big book, though.''

"Ever hear of anyone by the name of Sortino?" asked Shepard. "Victor Sortino?"

Connors thought a while. "Nope. Never heard of him.''

"Has this ever been a meeting place for really big card games — say a group of businessmen or gamblers?"

"Not that I know of. Lots of friendly little games. If

we knew about a big game, a regular one, we'd have busted it up. What are you driving at anyway, boy? You're not from the station, are you?"

"No," said Shepard. "Like I said — just a friend. But there's something I have to track down, tie up some loose ends. Tell me this — is it possible that around the time Kirby drew the money out of the bank he got into a big game in one of the rooms here? Poker?"

"I doubt it," said the house officer. "He wouldn't have had the time. Except for the night he quit early, he was always on the job. No, I think I'd have known it if he had been in a game with the customers."

"Well," said Shepard, "I can tell you this much. There were four men checked in here from out of town. A fifth one joined them and there was a poker game — the week Kirby was killed. Know anything of a five-man card game about that time?"

Connors was thoughtful. "Yes, there was a game that week — five men on. Wednesday or Thursday. Think it was a small game, not a big one. Looked that way."

"How do you happen to remember it?"

"Couldn't very well forget it," said Connors. "We had a complaint about a disturbance in that room — two rooms, really — a suite. Connecting bath."

"So what was it all about?"

"Well, someone called down and said there was a fight goin' on in one of those rooms — sounded like a couple of guys about to kill each other. I took Kirby along because I thought I might need help.

"There were five pretty hard-lookin' boys playin' poker. One claimed the others were cheatin' him. He was pretty well loaded and he took a poke at someone. We got that part listening outside. We both had pass-keys, and since there were two rooms I went in one and Kirby the other — both at the same time. Room I went in happened to be the one where the action was. They shut up quick enough when we told them to can it or get out.''

"You say they were hard-looking guys? Gangsters?''

"Well now, I wouldn't say that at all,'' said Connors, smiling. "Lot of hard-lookin' guys aren't gangsters. Half the joes who come in here look like they'd frighten their own mothers.''

"Poker game, huh?''

"Yeah.''

"Big stakes?''

"Don't know. They must have grabbed the bills. Didn't see anything but a few coins on the table.''

"Can you remember what any of these birds looked like?''

"Maybe. If I saw them again.''

"Was one of them a big-shouldered, tall guy — dark hair, dark skin, face like it was carved out of granite?''

"That could fit one of them. Give me some more.''

"Pocket eyes — like black ice in deep sockets. High cheekbones — like big knuckles under the skin. Face like petrified wood — all dead except the eyes.''

"Jesus, man! You must have just left him. That's the boy, all right. I'd remember him if I saw him twenty years from now. He must have come back from the Stone Age. How you happen to know a character like that?''

"It's too long a story,'' said Shepard. "And too un- believable. So you quieted them down and you left. Kirby right with you?''

"Yup. All the time — except when we first went in.''

"And that was the end of it? No more trouble?''

"None.''

"Where did Kirby go afterwards?''

"He relieved the man at the desk. Then he went to his office. He was there most of the night, far as I know.''

Now Shepard tried his hunch that there was some

link other than friendship between Kroger and Sortino. He took the snapshot of Kroger from his pocket and handed it to Connors. "Ever see this man before?" he said.

Connors inspected the picture carefully, then looked up in some amazement. "Sure," he said. "I've seen him. He's only the guy who started the beef over the cards, that's all."

Shepard contained his elation. He merely nodded. "He was definitely one of the five players, then?"

"Definitely one of the five," said Connors. "The loudest and the angriest. Listen — I should be asking you the questions."

"I'm just feeling my way," said Shepard. "Did Kirby show any sign of knowing these jokers when you entered those rooms?"

"No, sir. Not even by a look. I'd swear he didn't know one of them, nor they him."

"Were there any names mentioned?" asked Shepard. "I mean, did any one of the five speak to another player by name?"

"Well — let me think. . . . Yes, seems to me one of them called the other by name. Sounded like a last name, but I can't remember it."

"Was it Kroger?"

"Kroger? Sounds like it. But no — that wasn't it. The granite-faced one spoke to the guy that started the fight. Kroger is close to what he called him — but it was something else. I didn't pay much attention."

"Give it some thought," said Shepard. "It may be important. Meantime, tell me this — how did Kirby act after you left the room?"

"Nervous, preoccupied. But that wasn't unusual. Seemed like he was in a hurry to get back down to the lobby."

"When he left the hotel that night, was he carrying

anything — a suitcase, bag of some kind?"

"Don't know. Didn't see him leave."

"Can you think of anything else?"

"No, sir, that's it."

"Who else knew Kirby well here?"

"Only Mr. Bryant. He's one of the owners. Place used to be owned by Kirby's old man, you know."

"Yeah, I know. Where can I find Bryant?"

"California. He's out there visitin' with his sister."

"You think he'd know anything?"

"I don't think so. Usually he'd be up at his cottage this time of year — Candlewood Lake, Connecticut. But the poor man lost his missus a few weeks back and now he won't go near the place. Memories."

"Candlewood Lake did you say? In Connecticut?"

"That's right."

"Ever been there? To Bryant's place?"

"Just once. Mr. Bryant let me and the missus use it for a weekend. Took the kids, too. Very nice. Small house with about an acre of ground. Lonely for him with his wife gone and his son in the army."

"Did Kirby know about this cottage?" Shepard fought to conceal his excitement.

"Sure. I think he was there once or twice a long time ago. Anyway, he knew all about it."

"How long since anyone's used it?"

"Probably not since last spring. *Now* what's on your mind?"

"I'll tell you when I find out myself. How do you get there?"

"Well, you take the West Side Highway and you go on up to Saw Mill River Parkway and —" Connors paused, gave Shepard a sharp look. "I see what you mean," he said. "But if you were right, what would it prove?"

"Just tell me how to get there," said Shepard.

"I'll do better," the detective said. "I'll draw you a map." He took a loose-leaf notebook from his pocket and for a minute drew lines and landmarks, giving them labels. He explained the markings and gave the paper to Shepard.

Shepard stood up. The detective rose reluctantly and with a puzzled expression. Shepard stuck out his hand, and the detective took it firmly.

"Thanks one hell of a lot," said Shepard. "You've been a big help. Won't keep you any longer."

"That's all right," said Connors. "Hope you know what you're doin'. You need help, you ask for it. Remember, it's a rough world and this is a rough town."

"That it is," said Shepard. "One of the roughest towns in the whole rough world."

Connors looked thoughtful. "When you find the house," he said, "go around to the back. Over the door there's a heading a beam. It juts out a couple of inches. Reach up there and you'll find a key — or you will if Kirby put it back. I wouldn't want you to break in." He winked.

"Thanks," said Shepard. He gave the detective a small salute and walked decisively out of the building.

Chapter Eleven

Victor Sortino set down the book he was reading in the living room of Martin Kroger's Sutton Place apartment. He looked at his watch. It was twenty after three.

In another forty minutes Jake, Goldy, and Max would be on tap with the car. They'd damn well better be on time. The action would have to begin now — and fast!

Shepard, thought Sortino. Where did he come from? Who really sent him? Who is he? Cop? Possibly. The rugged build, the deceptively innocent college-boy face. If they were going to send men with sweet-boy faces, they should remember that the core of a man, hard or soft, was in his eyes. And in Shepard's eyes there was the cynicism, the cold-metal luster of the experienced, the unfrightened homicide cop.

Sortino was accustomed to measuring fear. He could smell it. He could feel it — and see it at a glance. He was in touch with the central animality of man. He could see the animal hiding there with bared teeth, crouched to spring — or with limp tail, cringing on whipped haunches. Shepard was in a cesspool of danger. And if he was cop, he would know it — and still be unafraid. But did he know? Did he even guess?

Unlikely, thought Sortino. What cop would come with a story like that? Or know enough to come at all?

The police would be sifting information from pigeons in side-street bars, seeking answers from possible witnesses and suspects in the back rooms of a precinct station. No, the law would not tip its hand with some crackpot story as bait for a juvenile trap. There was something else here, something entirely different.

It must be true then. It had to be the way he had figured it before he called the meeting. It couldn't be any other way.

Shepard wasn't a cop. His story was true — some of it, even most of it. A cop wouldn't come expecting to be asked for papers to prove his identity. And if he did come with phony papers, they wouldn't make him out as the landlord of a Florida apartment house. The police would give him local papers, a different business, and a better story. No, in some ways Shepard must be on the level. But the bastard was lying about the two hundred grand. He and the Kirby bitch knew exactly where it was. And in some connection that was beyond Sortino's comprehension, they had both been in with Kirby before he killed himself running with the loot.

Kirby must have given them a crazy, trumped-up story before he was killed. The guy got scared and dumped the money with them. Then he ran. Now Shepard, who must have been thick with the bitch all along, was trying to check out Kirby's story to see if the cash was cool — or hot from some heist. Kirby must have known his wife and Shepard were thick because he steered them to the wrong pigeon for the answers. He steered them to the very one they should be avoiding most. Revenge? Probably. But it didn't make any difference because Sortino would have caught on sooner or later. He was already far down the track. He had come to suspect. He had three aces of information and it would have been only a few days before he drew a full house.

There were lots of questions yet, but it didn't matter. He would get the answers wrapped around the two hundred thousand dollars.

After Shepard had left and Sortino had made a couple of phone calls, he had put all the pieces together and come up with a clear picture. They had been crossed all right. But not by Martin Kroger, alias Rick Trainor — it had been the night manager, Paul Kirby. One of those goddamn freaks where some boob stumbled onto a big pile and took a chance. All Sortino had to do was reconstruct that night at the Briteway and fill in a few blanks, guessing how it might have happened.

*T*he deal had taken shape in New York, but they had gone to Chicago to set it up. Max had been reading in the Sunday paper about a guy, a frog working out of a Paris jewelry house, who had just flown halfway around the world buying rare jewels from big potentates of little kingdoms. The jewels were supposed to be worth millions and the Frenchman had brought them to the American outlet in Chicago. The article said some of the jewels were merely on display, but others could be cut to order — if you had the price.

Sortino had recognized other possibilities.

The store had been thoroughly cased, the job well planned. A master of disguise — a necessity because Sortino's face was seldom forgotten — he had made himself into a somewhat ancient but distinguished-looking aristocrat. Then, posing as a big buyer, Sortino had excited the Frenchman into displaying his finest. Max, Goldy, and Jake, their faces masked, had entered precisely ten minutes behind him with drawn guns. There had been no bungling — alarms were silenced, clerks were tied in a matter of minutes, the valuable pieces were quickly identified and scooped up. The quartet vanished.

Some of the jewelry must have been moved to another store — because, when the carats were counted, the haul was figured just under a million.

The fence was one Rick Trainor — alias Martin Kroger — of 80 Sutton Place South. At the time only the bogus name was known to Sortino. Trainor was considered about the biggest buyer of stolen gems and stolen anything-of-value to his carefully screened customers. He was not yet known to the police, primarily, Sortino discovered later, because he covered himself with a legitimate and profitable loan company.

Sortino and his boys had let the job cool for a reasonable time, then had approached Trainor through contacts in New York. A meeting had been set up for an appraisal and sale at the little-known Briteway — Sortino, Goldy, Max, and Jake flying from Chicago and taking a suite of rooms there.

Trainor had turned out to be a real wise guy, very big stuff. He treated them like small-time mugs, amateurs who lifted hubcaps or rolled a few drunks and then fumbled their way into a big heist and came out smelling pretty. He acted like one of the big combine boys stepping down in class to buy a few trinkets as a favor to one of his mob. He was a wheel, he knew syndicate brass. He was supposed to be an international brain and hinted he could pick up a phone and make things happen anywhere in the world. So what? So he had connections and that made him a hero. He had a brave mouth.

Sortino and his boys had a few connections, too — and didn't need them. They had dropped out of the syndicate long ago. They were a team — neat, functional, careful. Probably they had stuck up their first bank when Trainor was still fencing ten-dollar junk in the back room of a store. Trainor was nothing to them. But they couldn't show it. He had something they wanted — dough. And they had the jewels they didn't want. So they had to sell him. They had to snow him under and butter him up. They pretended to be just about what he thought they were — cheap hoods, pushovers for a big shot like Trainor. They were meek little guys who bowed down, but — and this was a big but — quietly they had to let him see they knew a ten-carat stone from hunk of glass. And all the time they were fawning and playing it cozy, Trainor wasn't really getting away with anything.

Though he tried to conceal it, Trainor had been impressed with the jewels on that first night — but not with their marketability. They were too well known, too hot, and fine cutting was costly, he argued. There had been a lot of haggling over price, Trainor loud and abusive but finally agreeing painfully to two hundred thousand — an even fifty grand apiece.

Trainor returned the following evening carrying a brown satchel shaped liked a doctor's medicine bag, though somewhat larger. With him was a slight, swarthy man who had a foreign look and a trace of accent to match.

Both men produced the jeweler's eyepiece and again the gems were microscopically examined. They looked at each other, nodded, and the exchange was made. Drinks were passed, the deal toasted. Sortino asked Trainor if he would like to stay for a few rounds of poker. Trainor agreed readily, rubbing his hands together with pleasure.

However, before the game got underway, two things occurred. The money, in ten-thousand-dollar banded stacks of hundred dollar bills, was minutely examined and counted. Satisfied, Sortino placed the payoff in a small red leather overnight case. He then walked through the connecting bath to the adjoining room. He looked around for a place to hide the case, then decided the hell with it — Trainor would leave shortly, and they would make the split. He dropped the case on one of the twin beds.

Re-entering the room where a table was being set up for poker, Sortino was in time to see Trainor placing the jewels in the satchel and handing the bag over to the dark little man who had not been introduced and who hadn't spoken more than a few words. Trainor and the man now exchanged meaningful glances and the man departed immediately with the gems, never to be seen again.

Sortino did not question this. He knew nothing of Trainor, not even where he lived or how he operated. His New York contacts had briefed him that Trainor was a mysterious character and intended to remain so. The smallest question as to his methods, headquarters and associations, and he would bolt, the deal going with him. Sortino imagined that Trainor had reason to be careful. There were dishonest crooks who would make a last-minute switch or even hold up a fence and run with both money and loot.

Now fresh drinks were poured and cards were dealt. The poker game began. No chips were used, all pots were strictly cash. No limit was placed on the betting.

Trainor played skillfully, drew decent cards, and still won only two pots in as many hours. He was a shrewd businessman but a poor loser. As his roll drained away, so did his humor. He became sullen, sharp, accusatory. He increased his betting along with the alcohol in his drinks.

Soon, having lost eighteen grand, he was out of cash.

A stocky, balding man in his mid-forties, he turned to Sortino, the leader. In his high, crusty voice, he said, "I'm good for any amount, Sortino. I'll give you a check for another five G's."

Sortino's features were wooden. He gave his head

an almost imperceptible shake of negation. They had the dough for the jewels and could drop the pose. "Sorry," he said flatly. He spread his palms in a small gesture, signifying the hopelessness of the situation. "Of course, if we knew something about you, where you could be reached —"

Trainor's eyes rested on the stack of bills in front of Sortino. "You don't give a man a chance to get his money back, do you?" he said.

"Tomorrow," said Sortino, "is another day. Bring cash." He began to gather up his winnings. The others followed suit — Jake, massive with his blunt fighter's face; Max, thin and darkly dapper; Goldy, a tall bushy blond with the face of a chorus boy and the eyes of a reptile.

Trainor watched as the cash disappeared from the table into trouser pockets. The silence grew. Trainor chomped on his cigar while his face underwent a change of color. His eyes moved around the table and dropped to the picture of the nude on the top card of the pack in front of Sortino. Fifty-two nudes — all losers.

"You bastards ganged up on me," he said. "Lemme see that deck!"

Sortino picked up the deck and began to pass it. His hand hesitated, came back, and restored the cards to the table. He had no objection to showing the cards — but his honesty had been challenged.

"No," said Sortino. "We want to cheat you, we've got better ways. And quicker. For chrissake, if you can't take it, you better stick to bingo."

"Anytime I can't see the cards," said Trainor, standing up, "I know I've been rooked."

"Why you dumb sonofabitch," said Goldy, "you had the cards in your fat mitts, all night. Why didn't ya take a look at 'em?"

Trainor took the cigar out of his mouth and leaned

over the table, glaring in Goldy's face. "Listen, dimples," he growled, "don't give me any of that smart crap, or I'll ram it back down your throat!"

"Oh yeah?" said Goldy, half rising and looking slightly amused. "Put your fist where your mouth is. Or shut up." He sat down again with a satisfied grin.

Trainor dropped the cigar on the floor and stepped on it. He put one big ham on Goldy's shoulder and gave a gigantic backward shove. Goldy and the chair toppled over, both crashing loudly to the floor.

Goldy recovered and got up slowly. His eyes had a hooded, sleepy look. "That was a big mistake, pal," he said.

Everybody was watching with open-mouthed fascination — everybody but Sortino. His eyes were on Trainor, but his features were expressionless. He was taking the measure of Trainor's fear. There wasn't any — none at all. And that worried him.

Goldy advanced, a little crouched, hands loose at his sides, one wide shoulder dipping below the other, like a pitcher getting ready for the wind-up. He stopped squarely in front of Trainor. He waited.

Trainor swung heavily, but Goldy wasn't there. With a light dancing motion, he had sidestepped beautifully and flattened Trainor's ear with two jabs that sounded like the dribbling of a basketball. As Trainor stumbled sideways, Goldy followed and gave him a brutal kick in the rump. Now, as Trainor lay on the floor, Goldy raised his foot, about to squash his face.

"Okay, cut!" said Sortino. "The action's over, Goldy. Leave him alone."

Goldy backed off and was still laughing when Trainor rose with a vein of blood coursing from his ear, down his neck. He wiped it away with a handkerchief.

Strangely, Trainor now began to tinker with a fountain pen he had removed from his breast pocket.

For the first time, Sortino moved. He shoved the card table over and was across the room just as Trainor was bringing the pen up in what looked like a farcical attempt to aim it at Goldy as though it were a gun.

Sortino grabbed the arm and bent it around in back of Trainor until he screamed. Sortino released him and stepped away with the pen in his hand. He unscrewed the cap and tilted the barrel. Something dropped into his hand. He held it up toward Goldy.

"I'd say that was a thirty-eight caliber bullet," he said. "Your friend Trainor almost made you a present of it." He held up the long stem of the pen. "This part is the barrel, you see, Goldy? And the top is the firing assembly. You put them together and then you press down on this clip here. That's the trigger. Bingo! And they're dancing at your funeral."

"Jesus!" said Goldy. "What'll we do with the bastard now?"

"Let me have him," said Jake. "I'll beat him to death and toss him out the window. Suicide."

"Let him go," said Sortino. "After he killed Goldy, he would have been sorry. Wouldn't you, Trainor?"

"No," said Trainor. "But I did have one too many, I guess."

Sortino dropped the lethal fountain pen in his pocket. "You're lucky we don't kill just for kicks," he said. "Now get out of here before I change my mind."

"I've got to go to the can and straighten up," said Trainor. He was headed in that direction when there was a heavy pounding on the door.

"House officer, open up!" The muffled voice came from the corridor.

Sortino made a quick motion toward the card table. Max picked it up, Goldy gathered the cards wildly. Sortino dropped a few coins in the center of the table, and everybody sat down. Goldy dealt swiftly.

There was the sound of a key, then the door burst
open. The man in the gray suit, with the gray hair and
the preacher-boy face, appraised the room.

"Looks like a card game," he said. "Sounds like a
free-for-all in a bowling alley. What's the trouble here?"

"No trouble, officer," said Sortino. "Just a little
friendly dispute over who won the pot. Right, Trainor?"

Trainor mopped blood from his ear and nodded
assent.

"Didn't sound friendly at all," said the preacher-
boy cop. "Woman next door swears at least three people
were murdered."

"I don't see any bodies lyin' around," said Goldy.

"Why don't you shove it, Pop," said Max. "That
way you'll always have it."

"Shut up!" commanded Sortino. "The man's only
doing his job."

"That's right," said the house cop. "I don't want to
have to put you men out. But I will if —"

"What's going on here, Mike?"

The man in the brown suit could be seen standing
in back of Gray Suit and peering over his shoulder. He
was a real pretty boy trying to look official. Some two-bit
clerk, thought Sortino.

"Bunch of grown men squabbling over cards," said
the house cop. "Now keep the lid on, you guys. One more
complaint and you'll go out on your duffs."

"Blow it out, Pop," said Max under his breath. But
with a jangle of keys, the house cop had departed, taking
Pretty Boy with him.

"Next time, Max," said Sortino, "keep your mouth
shut. Some day you'll get the wrong house dick and he'll
smell out a bigger stink than just a little fight. If you're
sitting on a goddamn bomb, don't be tossing matches."

Max grinned, looked down at his nails. Trainor got
up and went to the can, shutting the door. There was the

sound of water running. After a while he came back looking combed out and meek.

"No hard feelings," he said to the room in general. "First time I let a half dozen hookers and a losing streak go to my head."

"You're lucky you've *got* a head," said Goldy.

"Beat it," said Sortino.

For a moment Trainor stood uncertainly, glancing from one to the other. Then he left the room.

"Sonofabitch might have killed me," said Goldy.

"'No hard feelings, fellas — the booze went to my head,'" mimicked Max in a perfect imitation of Trainor's hoarse squeal.

"Jesus!" said Jake. "What talent. You should of been a actor. If I wasn't lookin' at ya, I'd swear it was Trainor talkin'."

"Trainor?" said Max smugly. "He's easy. Sounds like a castrated frog with a sore throat."

"Let's see that gadget the pen," said Goldy.

Sortino passed it over and they all inspected it.

"How did you know?" said Goldy, handing it back.

"Old stuff," said Sortino. "Read the news. Keep up with crime." He lit a cigarette. "Anyone interested in the split? Or shall I keep it all for myself?"

"How about that?" said Jake. "The big pay-off. Honesty pays."

"Shuffle the greenbacks and deal them around," said Max. "I wanna see hundreds back to back."

A slight spasm tugged at the corners of Sortino's mouth. But the smile never came off. He went through the bath to the next room — and came thundering back.

"It's gone!" he said. "The whole pile. Anyone touch that bag on the bed?"

"Christ Almighty!" said Max. "No one left the room."

"Except Trainor," said Goldy. "Just now. He went

into the can.''

"He was running the water and he was gone a long time," said Jake. "He could of left the bag in the hall, then picked it up on his way out."

"He was plenty sore about losing his dough to the game," said Max.

In the silence that followed, Sortino was a statue growing ten feet tall.

"Come on," he said. "Let's go!"

Chapter Twelve

*T*rainor had just turned from paying off the taxi when they caught up with him. The street in front of the Sutton Place apartment house was deserted at that hour. Except for the soft splay of light from street lamps, it was dark. A cool breeze from the river carried pinpoints of distant sound. Otherwise the silence was immense.

Like drifting shadows, they fell in next to Trainor — two on either side.

Trainor looked up, startled. His mouth hung open to speak, but he said nothing. He must have caught the threat of danger in their vacant faces.

On one side, Goldy nudged Trainor's ribs with the big .45. On the other, the long blade of Max's knife drew blood below his armpit. Jake needed no weapon: His very size was a threat.

"Don't change your plans, Trainor," said Sortino. "Just invite us up for a drink."

Upstairs in 14-B, Sortino locked the door and drew the curtains. A single lamp had been burning and Sortino did not alter the lighting.

Goldy came out of one of the rooms, said, "It's okay, Vic. He's a loner."

Sortino nodded. He moved Trainor into a chair by the lamp. They grouped around him,

"What did you do with it?" said Sortino softly.

"Do with what?" said Trainor, recovering his former belligerence.

"I want to know where you hid the satchel with the two hundred grand after you swiped it from the hotel," said Sortino. "Don't play dumb with me, Trainor. You're out of your league."

"You're crazy!" said Trainor. "I gave you the dough. Do I have to guard it, too? If you can't hold onto it, why don't you hire a nursemaid?"

"Trainor," said Sortino evenly, "I can predict your future, you know that? You're going to be stubborn. You're going to hold out on us. And for that you're going to die."

"Yeah," said Goldy. "I can see it in his crummy eyes. He's gonna die. Slowly. In sections."

"Listen to this, you sneaky bastard," said Max. "Right from the crystal ball — You went in the can. You closed the door. You ran the water. Then you slipped into the other room, picked up the dough and opened the outside door. You took a chance. You put the case in the hall and then when you left you grabbed it again. You didn't think we'd catch up with you because we didn't know where you hung out."

"Yeah," said Jake. "That's the way it was, all right.

But he didn't have the dough when he got in the cab. So what did he do with it?"

"What did you do with it?" said Sortino. "Was the little guy who took the jewels waiting? Did you give the case to him?"

"You're out of your mind," said Trainor. "I don't play that way. I don't have to. If the cash is missing, one of your own boys took it and now he's trying to cover up."

"Search him," said Sortino.

Jake gave Trainor an open-handed swat across the side of the face. "Up!!" he said. Holding the livid cheek, Trainor stood. Max rifled his pocket, came up with apartment keys, handkerchief, some change, and a wallet. He went through the wallet.

"Six lousy bucks," he said. "An ident card and — a driver's license under the name of Rick Trainor, Brooklyn address."

"Why the Brooklyn address?" said Sortino.

"I use a lot of names and a lot of addresses," said Trainor, smiling and sitting down again.

"Look around and see what else you can find out about him, Goldy," said Sortino.

Goldy departed and returned in a minute with papers in his hand. "Found these in a desk," he said. "Letters to Martin Kroger, this address. Looks like our friend Trainor has a legit business under the name of Kroger. This guy has more handles than one of them Italian counts."

Sortino looked around, found the phone. He asked information for the number of the Briteway, then dialed. He got the room clerk.

"This is the police department," he said. "Sergeant Callahan, robbery detail. Were you on duty the last hour?"

"No, sir. Not all of it. Mr. Kirby relieved me for a while. I went out to eat. Got back a few minutes ago."

"Well, let me speak to whoever was on the last hour."

"Just a minute, sir."

In a moment, another man came on and said, "Yes, sergeant, can I help you?"

"You were on duty the last hour?"

"Yes, sir."

"We have reason to believe," said Sortino, "that a large sum of money, stolen in a robbery, might have been taken to the Briteway. Now, tell me this. In the last hour has anything been turned in at the desk to be kept in the safe? Anything at all? The name Rick Trainor might have been used."

"No, sir. Not a thing. Not under that name or any other."

"How about the check room? Small red leather case, a parcel, anything that would hold money."

"Just a moment, sergeant, I'll see."

The man came back. "Nothing," he said. "Not for two or three hours, they tell me."

"All right," said Sortino. "It may be we're on the wrong track. Unless we call you again, you can forget about it."

"Glad to help in any way we —"

"Thanks," said Sortino and hung up.

Sortino crossed the room and stood in front of Trainor.

"We're wasting time, Vic," said Goldy. "Let's go to work on the sonofabitch."

"You clean with the police?" said Sortino to Trainor. "Ever been booked, sent up?"

"Once I got a ticket for speeding," said Trainor smugly. "Two for parking." He smiled. "That's my complete record with the police. You think you're dealing with some ex-con?"

Sortino took the wallet from Max and examined it.

"What about this Brooklyn address? What's over there? And don't lie to me. We can check it out in no time."

"Wrong address," said Trainor. "It's a phony. So's the name. It's a precaution. I always take along phony papers when I go out on a deal like this."

Sortino unfolded a handkerchief and carefully wiped the wallet and all the papers that had been touched. Still holding it with the handkerchief, he ordered Trainor to stand, then placed the wallet in his hip pocket.

"I'll take the keys to the apartment," he said to Max. "I like this place. Very nice. Well furnished, too. You have a lease, Trainor?"

"I own it," said Trainor. "Cooperative."

"That's even better," said Sortino.

"For chrissakes, Vic," said Goldy. "When are we gonna sweat him?"

"Not here," said Sortino. "Over at Jake's, in the basement." He looked at his watch, then at Trainor. "Unless he talks, I want him dead in one hour. First, I want to hear screams and I want to see a lot of blood."

"We ain't gonna disappoint you," said Jake. "You'll think you're in a Chicago slaughter house."

Sortino looked at Trainor. Again he was taking the measure of fear. He saw hate, worry — but no fear. Sortino didn't like it. Not at all. He didn't think Trainor would talk. They were going to have to kill him.

A naked bulb glared from the ceiling as they stood around Trainor, who was rope-tied to a chair. In front of him was a heavy workbench, into which had been driven five widely spaced nails. Each finger of Trainor's hand had been securely fastened to the bench by wire, one finger to a nail. Goldy had brought the short, heavy-bladed ax and was standing by with it, a pleased grin on his face.

"Maybe," said Sortino speculatively, "we could persuade him first with Jake's fist. I don't know. I don't think anything simple like that is going to work with this one. But we could try." Sortino had the slightly puzzled look of a professor who is struggling with a weighty problem in physics. "Show him what he can expect, Jake."

Jake doubled one giant hand into a sledge=hammer fist and held it in front of Trainor's nose.

"Jesus!" said Max. "I'd rather be hit with a pile driver."

"It's a beautiful weapon, Trainor," said Sortino, tapping the fist with his forefinger. "With one blow your nose would be as boneless as custard. You might find a surgeon who could rebuild it. But it would never look the sate." He shook his head sadly. "Never."

"I don't get it," said Trainor. "You know I didn't steal it back from you. So what do you want? Another ten grand? I'll deal with you."

"All or nothing," said Sortino.

"Twenty," said Trainor.

"Jake," said Sortino.

Jake drew back the fist and accurately, with one powerful jab, flattened Trainor's nose. Trainor, in groaning agony, held his nose with his free hand.

"You want me to cave in his mouth now?" said Jake. "No," said Sortino, "I want to be able to hear him talk. Where did you hide the money, Trainor?"

Trainor spat blood at Sortino. "You dirty gutter rat bastard," he said "I'm gonna hunt you down and kill you!"

Sortino wiped blood from the lapel of his coat, cleaning, it away fastidiously with a handkerchief.

"You know," he said, "money is a relative thing. If

you've got it, it isn't very important.'' He held up his
finger. ''If I had your money, I wouldn't trade this for
fifty grand. And I wouldn't trade the other four for two
hundred thousand. But you're gonna lose ten fingers and
ten toes in the next ten minutes at ten thousand apiece
if you don't talk.'' He sighed. ''Max, be ready with the
tourniquet and plenty of bandages. We can't have him
bleed to death. Not yet. Goldy, you set?''

"Ready, Vic.'' Goldy raised the ax and took a careful
sight on Trainor's little finger, the smile spreading over
his face.

"No!'' said Trainor. ''I didn't do it. I didn't do it!
But I'll scrape up another two hundred grand in the
morning. I'll even get the gems back.''

"No credit,'' said Sortino.

"In God we trust,'' said Max.

"I want to know where you hid that money,'' said
Sortino. ''Now!''

"I didn't do it. My God, you've got to believe me. I
didn't. I didn't!''

Sortino looked at Goldy, shrugged, gave a small,
tight nod. Goldy lifted the ax higher. It gleamed for a
moment, came down swiftly, surely.

Trainor screamed — a high, thin wail, rising and
falling, echoing back from the shadows of the basement
cavern. . . .

*R*emembering now, with the added knowledge that
Trainor had been telling the truth after all, Sortino felt
slightly uncomfortable. It had been a very grim night.
Goldy's talents had been called for again and again. It
had been useless. Sortino had finally lost patience and,
grabbing the ax, had delivered the fatal blow himself.

They had buried the body miles away in a field by

a wooded area. Had not a gang of grade-school boys been digging trenches for mock warfare a week later, it might never have been found. Still, it was about as unrecognizable a corpse as could be dug up anywhere — mutilated features, fingerless hands eliminating telltale prints. They had left Trainor's wallet in his pocket, empty of all but a typewritten identification card giving the phony name and the address of a Chinese laundry in Brooklyn. If the body was ever discovered, it had amused them to think that the police would be chasing false leads. But looking back now upon the unnecessary risk of Trainor's killing, it was not very funny at all.

From letters, memos and other papers they found later in Kroger's apartment, Sortino learned about the loan company, Kroger's frequent trips to Europe, and that during his last absence he had let a friend use the apartment. Perfect! With Max's talent for imitation, Sortino would know how to put that information to good use.

Carefully instructed by Sortino, Max got on the phone to Louise Buckley and, pretending to be calling from the airport, did a marvelous imitation of Kroger's high, grating voice. The next call was placed to the super at 80 Sutton Place South. Max said that he, Martin, Kroger, was taking a sudden and extended business trip to Europe. He might even be gone a year. Meanwhile, he was turning the apartment over to his good friend and business associate — Mr. Victor Sortino — who was to receive all mail and decide what should be forwarded.

There had been no trouble. The super was quite understanding. After the killing and disposal of the body, there did seem to be an excellent purpose in moving to Kroger's apartment. For one thing, Sortino was then positive that Kroger had passed the money to an accomplice — probably the foreign little man who had gone away with the jewels. Not knowing that Kroger was dead, the dark little man might come right up to the apartment with the two hundred grand — or the knowledge of it and fall into a trap. But in case the little man inquired after Kroger in the lobby and left in high suspicion, Sortino would have his boys watching outside in shifts twenty-four hours a day, until it seemed hopeless.

Further, Sortino would have access to Kroger's incoming mail and phone calls, screening the latter carefully and keeping Max on tap to play Kroger at the first sound of an accented voice. Thus, a neat trap could be set up to recover the money and, with luck, the jewels as a bonus.

Lastly, it had pleased and amused Sortino to take over the dead man's apartment as a sort of posthumous revenge. And the scale of living was much more to his liking. Maybe some angle would present itself in which he would be able to take for himself other of Kroger's assets and eventually rise to a similar position of wealth and prestige. But finally, it seemed to Sortino that the last place in the world the police would look for Kroger's murderer, if the body were by some impossible freak discovered and identified, was in his own apartment. Especially since Kroger himself, played by Max, had made the apartment available to his friend, Sortino. Anyway, by the time the police could unravel so involved a situation, Sortino would be long gone.

Until this moment, almost everything had fouled up. Neither the little foreigner nor any other prospect who seemed connected with him or Kroger's fencing operation dead shown. The mail had revealed nothing, the phone calls had been from people associated with the loan company or friends who seemed in the clear. Louise Buckley had come around to the apartment, appearing in some subtle way to be slightly suspicious and nervous. Something might have to be done about her. And then the body had been discovered, though not identified as Kroger.

There were only two other people who could possibly have stolen the money — the house dick or the pretty boy in the brown suit. Since Brown Suit had arrived on the scene late and the detectives had the passkey, Sortino figured that the latter must have stolen the money, entering the adjoining bedroom first and quietly making off with it before the show of authority.

Convinced, Sortino had sent Goldy to shadow the detective and check on everything about him. After a few days, Goldy had reported that the detective had led him exactly nowhere, deposited no sums of money, spent no large amount, lived on the same mediocre scale you would expect of him. Unless the guy was cleverer than Goldy thought, he was clean.

Now, although Sortino did not even remember Kirby's name and was unaware of his death, he had been about to have Goldy track down everything about him. Had not Shepard arrived on the scene, Goldy would have been on the trail the next day.

But now Sortino had a nearly complete picture of what had really taken place at the Briteway. It was clear enough. When the house dick had entered the room in which they were playing poker, the night manager, Kirby, had, at the same moment, investigated the adjoining room. The money case had been on the bed, unlocked. He had opened it. The sight of all that green had overpowered him. Making a quick decision, he had sneaked out with the case and hidden it in a linen closet or mop room — any place where he could lay hands on it in a hurry. Then he had stepped in behind the house dick and played dumb. Later he had chickened out and turned the money over to his wife and Shepard, running scared for the hills after telling a trumped-up story of how he got the two hundred grand. He must have matched Sortino with the name on the register. Why he had given the name to Shepard and where he had been going when he was killed didn't matter. Now Sortino had to get the money back fast, one way or another, and beat it out of town before trouble closed in.

At five minutes to four, Sortino went to the kitchen and made a quartet of powerful drinks. There would be just one drink each, but it would give them plenty of guts for the task.

He had taken the drinks on a tray to the study when the bell rang. He went to the door, opened it.

"Right on the button, boys," he said.

Goldy, Max, and Jake stepped in, closing the door quietly and following Sortino into the study where the latter served the drinks and waited silently behind the desk.

"What's the deal, Vic?" said Goldy. "Sounds like you're onto somethin' big. We got the noise from Jake."

Sortino leaned back and built a pyramid with his fingers. His eyelids came to half-mast in the solid glacier of his face.

"Gentlemen," he pronounced, "we are only human. We make mistakes. As in the case of Rick Trainor — God rest his soul."

Goldy snickered but Sortino gave him a look and he subsided instantly.

"Trainor was an honest man," Sortino went on. "He acted in good faith. As they say in the courts, he was hung on a rope of circumstantial evidence."

"He got it shoved in and broken off, all right," said Max.

"Now," said Sortino, ignoring Max, "there's nothing we can do about Trainor."

"Man!" said Jake, reverently. "All the king's horses —"

"All the king's horses," said Sortino. "Quite right. Very astute of you, Jake. But please shut your goddamn mouth until I'm finished. All of you!"

He waited until the faces became vacant of expression again.

"With a little luck and a lot of brainwork," he continued, "I have put together what really happened that night. Not only do I know who stole the two hundred grand, I also have a pretty good idea how to get it back. There are two people in this town who know where the money is hidden. They can be made to talk. And afterwards, they can be made silent."

"I'm ready," said Goldy. "Let's hear some names, Vic."

"Yeah," said Jake. "And some places. Where do we begin?"

For the second time that day, Sortino removed from his wallet the piece of paper upon which the Kirby address and phone number had been written. "We begin with a call," he said. "To see if our party is at home."

Watching their faces, he lifted the receiver and began to dial rapidly.

Chapter Thirteen

It was going on five o'clock when Shepard left the Briteway. At the subway entrance he paused and changed his mind. He looked around for a drugstore, found one, and went in. He called Corinne.

"No time for cute conversation, sweetheart," he said. "I'm on to something — a terrific lead. Now listen, do you have a car?"

"Yes. The insurance company replaced the one that was wrecked."

"Good. Where is it?"

"In a garage near here. I don't use it much."

"Okay — go get it. And be parked in front of your apartment house in twenty minutes. Can you do that?"

"Yes. It's only a couple of blocks. Am I going with you? And where?"

"Connecticut is where. And I'd better go alone. Don't know what I might run into." He was thinking that anything could happen to a man who might be carrying two hundred thousand dollars in cash. And that reminded him that he had better make another stop — at a pawnshop — or any place where they sold guns.

"Connecticut!" said Corinne. "Does that mean you know where Paul —"

"It means that I might know and I might not. Don't get your hopes up."

"Don't get my hopes up! Over two hundred thousand dollars? Neil, darling, take me with you. Please? I couldn't stand the waiting and wondering."

"Sorry, baby, but no can do. I'll be on the go every minute, and it could get complicated with two of us. Besides I don't know anything for sure. It's all guesswork. I'll give you the complete scoop on everything when I get back."

"What time do you think that will be?"

"I don't know exactly. Probably not before one or two in the morning. No earlier."

There was a silence. "Listen, darling," she said. "I don't feel like being alone. A girl friend called and asked me to dinner. I said I couldn't, but think I will now. I'll taxi over and stay for the evening."

"Fine. I'd rather you weren't alone. And listen, on second thought, I might be a little late getting up there. Have to make another stop. You go along."

"What about the car?"

"Park it in front of the building and leave the keys under the seat, driver's side. What does it look like?"

"Fifty-four Cadillac convertible — yellow with a black top."

"Okay, I couldn't miss that one. You go ahead."

"If you're sure you don't mind."

"I don't mind."

Silence.

"Darling," she said. "I — I've been thinking all afternoon. Maybe you ought to drop the whole thing and go on back to Florida."

"Why?"

"Because I never have been and probably never will be anything but trouble for you."

"Don't talk like that, sweetheart."

"No — don't stop me. Because it would be the first decent thing I've done in a long time — to let you out. And it wouldn't take a puff of wind to make me change my mind. And everything I want is planned and calculated. Even now — right at this minute I'm . . . oh, never mind. You'd better just forget about me, Neil. If I don't bring trouble it happens wherever I am. It's the same thing."

"I don't know," he said. "Maybe you're a lot of things. But I can't seem to care — because I love you. Besides, I'm selfish enough myself to want fifty thousand dollars bad enough to stick my neck out. So don't worry about it."

"Well — if you put it that way. Are you sure?"

"Sure."

"All right then, darling. Bring mama the bacon and we'll cut you a piece. I told you it wouldn't take much to change my mind."

"I'll see you then, honey."

"Be careful. And I'll be waiting at home for you."

"Better not wait up."

"I'll put my spare key on the ring with the car keys."

"Okay, sweetheart. Got to run. 'Bye."

He hung up.

*T*he traffic was heavy on the West Side Highway. Tight clusters of suburbanite commuters pushed homeward in an angry snarl of mortgaged metal. Right and left, fore and aft, Shepard could see nothing but the scurry of anonymous vehicles. But ten miles out on the Saw Mill River Parkway traffic thinned, spaced itself more comfortably. And Shepard relaxed.

On the seat beside him was the map Connors had drawn of the approach to Candlewood Lake. In his pocket was the snub-nosed secondhand .38 revolver he had just bought, and in his mind a hum of thoughts to match the quiet drone of the yellow Cadillac.

The gun, thought Shepard, was perhaps unnecessary. If he came back with the money, his protection was in the secrecy of its possession. But the .38 was small comfort in a situation containing infinite possibilities for trouble. There were still too many unanswered questions.

*F*ive minutes after he left Danbury, Connecticut, just a few miles from Candlewood Lake, Shepard began to worry about the persistent glare of headlights from a lone car behind him. The car was well back, never gaining on him, and ordinarily it would have been silly to give it a second thought. But under the circumstances of his mission imagination gave that single pacing car exaggerated importance. A slight current of uneasiness overcame him every time he glanced in the rear-view mirror. Finally he put on a burst of speed, and when the car still made no attempt to gain ground he felt easier.

Rounding a curve, the lone car became invisible. Now, consulting the map, he turned onto a narrow, winding road that would take him directly past the cottage. For insurance, he drove a few hundred feet down this road, then pulled to the edge and cut his lights. In the pitch-darkness he watched and waited. A minute or two later when the car went on by without making the turn, he dismissed it entirely as a tail. Amused now at his overconcern, he pulled the light switch and moved forward again.

The road was so narrow that two cars could not pass each other without tight maneuvering. The area surrounding it was completely wooded, the trees so dense that they formed a bower that nearly blacked out the sky above. The houses were widely separated, mostly unlighted and set well back from the road. In the darkness the lake below could not be seen at all.

After a mile of torturous dipping and turning, Shepard began to inspect mailboxes with a flashlight he had found in the glove compartment. In high excitement he discovered the one marked JAMES R. BRYANT a quarter mile beyond. Again he cut his lights and waited. When after a reasonable time the road behind remained in total darkness, he turned into the drive.

The cottage, set back about a hundred yards from the road, was a small two-storied affair with a wood-frame-and-stone exterior. Shepard parked the car beside it and, switching off the lights, made his way to the rear with the flashlight.

He paused at the door, listening. There was the faint rustle of leaves from the overhang of trees, the thin distant whine of an outboard — nothing else. Miles away, from a high-flung point that must overlook the opposite side of the lake, a lonely house, like a great sleepy cat, peered down with yellow eyes.

Shepard reached above him, found the extended edge of beam, and ran his hand along it. He couldn't find the key. Then he tried again and came across it far to the left. He illuminated the lock, turned key and knob until the door opened. He stepped in, closed and locked the door behind him.

He was in the kitchen. He wondered if he should chance an experiment with the light switch to see if the electricity was turned on. He decided that searching with a flashlight would be too difficult and, since the house was far removed from neighbors, he could gamble on it. He found the switch and an overhead fixture glared with light.

He gave the kitchen only a passing examination and went on to the living room. Here he found a massive fieldstone fireplace, a confusion of maple furniture, a scattering of worn throw rugs. The walls were knotty pine, the ceilings high with exposed beams. It was about what you would expect of a lake cottage — crude and rustic, with utilitarian furniture. A wide picture window that must look down from the crest of the hill upon the lake in daylight now saw only vague shadows in the opaque beyond.

To his surprise Shepard found the room, though deep in dust, in complete order. Somehow he had expected to see some evidence that Kirby had been there, leaving in his confused state of mind a tray full of butted cigarettes, a whisky-smelling glass, or a half-eaten sandwich. Nothing of the sort. The place was quite tidy. Disappointed, he immediately began to wonder if his hunch was wrong.

He poked around in the living room, even peering up the chimney without reward. He was turning away from the fireplace when he saw some shards of glass behind a small pyramid of logs, he removed a log and bent down. The shattered glass had once enclosed a fifth of whisky. Satisfied that only Kirby would have flung the bottle there, Shepard smiled and began to search with real spirit.

There was a single bedroom downstairs. This was also neat and barren. Likewise, the bathroom. Shepard mounted stairs to what was more an enclosed balcony overlooking the living room than a bedroom. There was just space for twin beds, a lamp and table, and a cur-tained clothes rack. One of the beds was smoothly made, while the other was careless and lopsided. On the floor, just under the bed, he found a much-used, heavily stained paper cup. It smelled faintly of whisky and contained a shredded cigarette butt.

This was where Kirby must have slept that Friday night.

After looking around fruitlessly for the case contain-ing two hundred thousand dollars, Shepard sat down on the bed.

It seemed obvious to him now that Kirby would not hide the money in the house. Even though cleverly concealed, it might still be found by some accident. Further, if Bryant loaned or rented the house, the money would be inaccessible. Therefore, it must be hidden someplace on the grounds where it could be reached even while the house was occupied.

Returning the house to darkness and the key to its place, Shepard took a rocky path and began a careful descent to the lake. The torch cut strange shadows out of the night and a silence like breathless waiting closed in around him.

Near the edge of the lake there was a padlocked bathhouse. There was also a boathouse and this, too, was locked. But the boathouse contained a tiny window that could be opened by inserting the arm through a half broken pane of glass and turning the latch.

Shepard was about to gull himself over the sill when, above the whispered mutterings of the night, he heard what sounded like the muted snap of a car door closing.

He froze, cut the torch, and listened. His hand stole around the butt of the .38 in his pocket.

The rasp of metal-on-metal had seemed to come from the road beyond the house. But there was total darkness above, and the sound was not repeated, thought he waited a long time. It might have been anything. And in such stillness, echoed from a greater distance than he imagined.

He squeezed inside the boathouse. But before making light, he covered the small window with his coat. Now, still listening, he sent a cone of brilliance over the objects around him.

Paddles, oars, and other boating paraphernalia clung by brackets to the rough walls. There was a canoe and, beside it, about fifteen feet of fiberglass boat with an old twenty-five-horse Johnson outboard at the stern. The shed didn't look like it could conceal much of anything, but Shepard searched until he was sure. Then he saw a ladder that ascended to a platform containing more equipment and just plain junk. Following the beam of his flashlight, Shepard climbed the ladder.

For a time he browsed around in the litter of life preservers, rubber floats, paint cans, tools, and fishing tackle. Nothing. But in a corner there was a high, square, boxlike protrusion. It turned out to be a heavy wooden cover, and, when Shepard lifted it with much heaving, he found a gas motor with an exhaust pipe leading to the exterior. It was either a pump to get water from the lake or an emergency generator. It didn't matter. Nothing there, either. Hardly room to squeeze in a lunchbox, let alone a suitcase.

Shepard began to replace the cover and, in doing so, noticed that the motor sat on a small dais, the boarded side of which closed the area beneath from view. Quickly he set the cover down and felt around the structure until he came to an opening. He reached in and when he touched canvas, he pulled. Slowly a small section of tarpaulin was exposed — and what came with it was heavy. Bursting with anticipation, he tugged with both hands until he had the thing resting at his feet.

He unwrapped the tarpaulin, revealing an imitation red leather suitcase!

His fingers awkward from nervous excitement, Shepard unlatched and opened the case.

Two banded stacks of hundred-dollar bills fell out of the green overflow to the floor. Fascinated, he picked them up and examined them closely. Satisfied, overjoyed, he tossed the stacks in with the others. Obviously Kirby had intended to come back for the money in a matter of days. It was only a good temporary hiding place. Shepard studied the outside of the case but could find no initials. On impulse, he dumped the entire contents on the floor. All the money looked genuine. He felt around in the cloth pockets of the case. They were empty.

He was glad because now he wasn't sure he wanted the case to tell him anything. And yet he knew the case didn't belong to Kirby. He had asked Corinne, and she said she had never seen it before. Kirby had explained that he had borrowed it from a resident hotel employee. But Shepard could never quite swallow that — any more than he could accept the fact that those five men had carried two hundred thousand dollars in cash, all hundreds, among them.

The interior lining of the case was slightly torn at one corner. And around the corner, the material looked too full. He stuck his hand through the opening under the lining, tearing it still more. His fingers touched paper, withdrew a yellow folded square. He opened it and discovered a telegram. The telegram was addressed to a Chicago hotel and read:

BUSINESS CONFERENCE SET FOR BRITEWAY HOTEL TO-MORROW NIGHT 9 P.M. READY TO CLOSE DEAL IF MER-CHANDISE AND PRICE SATISFACTORY.

— RICK TRAINOR

Shepard frowned. Rick Trainor — the name rang a loud bell of danger. Rick Trainor! Of course! That was the name of the mutilated corpse with the phony papers. And so Rick Trainor — had been one of the five at the game. But he must have come, not to play poker primarily, but to buy some merchandise — merchandise worth two hundred thousand dollars. And unless the money later entered the game, a very doubtful possibility, it probably had been stolen from Trainor or whoever had sold the merchandise and received nearly a quarter of a million dollars in payment.

If you guessed that the merchandise was something highly illegal then you could understand why Sortino would keep his mouth shut. Sure! And he might have a second reason, an even better one — to recover the money without giving warning by showing his interest in it.

Shepard tossed the green hoard back in the case, slammed the cover, and snapped it shut. After he got the money to a safe place, he would worry about where it came from and to whom it really belonged. Until then, it was Corinne's — except for fifty thousand dollars.

My God, he thought. Why did I come equipped with too much curiosity and a built-in conscience?

He replaced the motor cover and went down the ladder. He doused the light and got his coat. Now he opened the window and stood for a minute listening. The silence was just as unnerving as sound. He dropped the case to the ground and followed it, closing the window, locking it.

This time, after adjusting his eyes to the darkness, he groped his way up the path without light. He approached the convertible, pausing to listen and watch. It seemed safe, so he took the gun from his pocket and stole behind it to the car door. He gave a quick pulse of light to the interior of the Cadillac. Nothing.

He took the keys from his pocket, went around, and opened the trunk, locking the case inside. He swung behind the wheel and was about to flip the key when, from above, headlights flared around a turn, dancing beams off the trees and spraying past in a blur of light and shadow too fast for the narrow, twisting road.

Shepard sighed, plucked the gun from the seat, and dropped it in his pocket. Probably some drunk hurrying to his own accident. Still, when he fired the motor, Shepard moved out onto the road without lights, crawling until he was some distance from the house before pulling the switch. He would have been happier if the speeding car had not been headed as he was, back to the highway. He supposed that darkness and two hundred thousand dollars would conspire to make anyone jumpy — even if the money had no hidden strings of complication.

He gained the highway without incident. And, although several cars followed and others passed him from time to time on the way to Danbury, it was on the other side of the city that he became certain he was being tailed.

Chapter Fourteen

*I*t was going on eleven o'clock. At this hour the road that Shepard traveled was nearly deserted. And yet for miles a lone car clung to him, a quarter mile back at every turn. When Shepard slowed, the car behind did likewise. When he gunned to dangerous speeds, his tail was there, always the same distance away, preserving the quarter-mile separation.

Several ideas — including sudden turn-offs, U-turns and other tricks — occurred to Shepard, but he didn't like any of them. Then, when he saw the lights of a café ahead, he thought of a better plan.

First he slowed. Then as he came abreast of the place, he turned in suddenly, pulled up in the shadows of the parking area, and waited, lights out.

In a few moments, his tail sped into view and, as Shepard had hoped, went past. He tried to identify the make of car and its passengers. He could do neither — the lights blinded him, and then the dark body went by too fast.

Immediately Shepard leaped out and opened the trunk, removing the case. He went to the front of the car and looked around. He was against one windowless wall of the building, and it was semi-dark — no one was watching him.

He felt for the catch that released the hood. It

clicked and he lifted. He had been thinking about it when he picked up the tail, and he already knew the exact spot — in the area to the right of the motor and just in back of the generator. He had noticed the hiding place on the way up when he had stopped for gas and watched the attendant check the oil and water.

He placed the case horizontally into the empty space, and the fit was snug, but good. He closed the hood and it came down easily without forcing. He backed out quickly and brought the convertible to the more strongly lit front of the building. From where he was now parked, he could see through a window to the bar that ran parallel to it. If he sat on one of the stools in the gloom, he could swing sideways and observe the Cadillac clearly. He locked the car and went inside.

The room was small and narrow, with dark-stained wood paneling and a dusky atmosphere. Beyond Shepard could see a longer room, with square tables bearing red-and-white checkered cloths. This room was deserted.

There were only three people at the bar — a young couple sitting at one end and, at the other, a paunchy little man who was drinking boilermakers and watching through a boozy haze a late movie on the overhead television screen. Shepard took a seat about center and ordered a bourbon and soda, which was served to him by a gray-haired, blowzy woman in a soiled apron.

Now Shepard swung his stool so he could look out upon the Cadillac and the highway beyond. Several cars whizzed by in both directions. But in five minutes, none had stopped.

Meantime, Shepard had a shuddering, imaginary picture of Rick Trainor's mutilated, disfigured corpse. He knew now that he was playing in a game where not only cards were stacked — but also bodies. The excitement had gone. He wanted out, but he didn't know how to get there.

He began to wonder what Trainor had done to deserve his end. The answer was forming in his mind when a dark Buick sedan approached from the direction in which Shepard had just come, braked, turned into the parking lot, and pulled up beside the convertible.

Two men got out but did not give the yellow Cadillac so much as a glance. That was a relief to Shepard since the car had come from the wrong direction to be the tail — though it could have gone by again, then swung back.

In any case, Shepard did not like the look of the men. Their style of dress was a little too natty for local types, and they moved shoulder-to-shoulder with a relaxed purposefulness and sullen power.

Together they entered the bar, giving Shepard his first decent look at them.

His attention was taken immediately by the bigger one. He was tall and immense. His arms were long and his meaty hands, like his blunt pitted face, spoke of crushing fights — both in street and ring. His facial expression was blank.

The blond one was nearly as tall, but of a loose hardness and wiry structure. His features were as smooth as the other's were craggy. The face had a boyish wickedness and contempt — but the eyes held an ancient evil.

For a moment, the two paused at the edge of the room, sizing it up in a quick glance. Their eyes rested on Shepard no longer than on the others, and with the same impersonality.

Now they moved casually toward the center of the bar and, as they reached Shepard, separated and mounted stools on either side of him, the big one on his right, the blond one left.

"Set up a beer for me, Mom," said the blond.

"Make that two," said his massive friend.

Both looked straight ahead.

The blowzy woman, having seen them enter together, looked from one to the other in some amazement. Then she must have caught something in the very air that made her turn quickly and fill the order.

Down the bar, the young couple talked, oblivious, while the paunchy drunk at the other end watched the television screen with stupid attention.

At first Shepard had the frightened feeling of the bad end of something that should never have been begun. The feeling drained and was replaced by a distorted relief at coming to grips with the enemy. And, finally, he felt a growing sense of anger.

The anger was brought about by the smug, invincible quality in the actions of the two men. They had come into the bar and flanked him without a word, like soldiers impervious to reprisal in taking an enemy caught behind their own lines. The pride and fear of the cornered animal in Shepard made him want to strike back with quick brutality. He could smash Blondy in the face with the swift hammer of his fist and, with luck, still bring the gun to bear on Muscles.

But he fought the urge. It would be a dangerous move because it was built on emotion. He had to think and act as coolly and deliberately as they did — and still not weaken his force with fear. So he only waited and pretended — if not ignorance — indifference.

"Not many customers tonight, eh, Mom?" said Blondy, sipping his beer.

"Nah," she said. "Still too early in the season. Another month and we'll be full up all the time."

"Yeah," said Blondy. "So you're all alone here, Mom? No help?"

She nodded her head, wiping a glass with a dirty towel. "My husband — he's sick in bed. But tomorrow he's all right again."

"Yeah, sure. But what good does that do you to-night?"

Her eyes widened. She looked a little frightened. "I don't know what you mean, mister," she said.

"I mean, suppose someone comes with a big gun —" he mocked a thumb and forefinger "— and takes all the cash."

She laughed nervously. "Not much cash to take," she said, adding defensively, "Besides, I'm not alone." She looked around. "These people are here."

"People!" snorted Blondy. "What people? You call these people? Are they fighters? What you got here? A pot-bellied drunk, a couple of punk kids and —" For the first time he turned slightly towards Shepard. "— And this one here. I don't know *what* he is. Are you a fighter, George?"

Shepard turned until he was looking Blondy in the eye. "Maybe," he said. "If I were, could you find me someone to fight?"

"Sure thing, George," said Blondy. He eyed the big one slyly. "How about him?"

"Oh," said Shepard, "can he fight?"

"He can fight, George."

"Maybe you could introduce me to him," said Shepard. "And then we could put on the gloves and go a couple of rounds together."

"I could do that," said Blondy with a twist of smile, "and you wouldn't even need gloves."

The big one, who had been passively sipping his beer, was now looking down at the clenched fist of one hand, cocking his head in a listening attitude.

"Well, if you could introduce us, then you know him. That right?"

"That's right, George."

"Then if you know him," said Shepard, "why don't you haul your carcass over there and sit next to him like a good friend?''

There was a silence while all the fun seeped out of Blondy's face.

"Listen, mister," said the female barkeep to Blondy, "you trying to make trouble in here?''

"Keep your drawers on, Mom," said Blondy. "Just a little private chuckle." With that he lapsed into silence.

Shepard finished his drink and paid for it. Now comes the test, he thought, and climbed off the stool.

As he began to walk toward the door, he saw from the corner of his eye that the blond one was tossing a bill on the counter and that the big one was on his feet. He wasn't halfway across the room when they both came up behind him.

His hand itched for the gun in his pocket. But somehow he was positive that, however casual or sudden the move, he would be too late. He decided that Muscles was mighty impressive, but he would have to deal with Blondy first.

Outside, there wasn't time to conceal his movements because they fell in beside him right away. He didn't say anything. There wasn't anything to say and everybody knew it. He walked over to the car and a single clever move still hadn't occurred to him. He would have to play it by ear all the way.

When his fingers touched the door handle, the blond one said quietly and in an all-business-now tone, "I'll take the keys, George."

Shepard turned. "What makes you think I'll give them to you?''

"This," said Blondy. The big blue-steel .45 came into his hand as Muscles stepped close to shield it from view of the café.

Shepard reached into his pocket, felt the gun. He looked into Blondy's eyes and changed his mind. He brought out the keys and dropped them in the out-stretched hand.

Blondy gave the keys to the other and said, "Take a good look inside, Jake. Then check the trunk." He pulled the .45 in close and turned his back on the café.

"Right, Goldy," said Jake. They were the first words he had spoken. Now he fumbled with the keys and got the door open. He made a thorough search. "Nothin'," he said and went to the trunk. He came back shaking his head. "Clean. He never had it or he dumped it."

"What did you do with it, George?" said Goldy.

Shepard could think of some answers but they wouldn't be smart. He decided to play it straight. "I'm not going to kid you," he said. "But let's make sure we're talking about the same thing. What is it I'm supposed to have?"

"Two hundred thousand bucks cash," said the one called Goldy.

Now Shepard thought he should take a chance, on one smart answer with a purpose — a hook. "I gave it to Sortino," he said.

They looked at each other, "Let's take him somewhere and bruise him a little," said Jake.

Goldy ignored him. "I thought you weren't gonna kid me, George." He still spoke softly, almost amiably. "You're gonna give the dough to Sortino, all right. In the end, you're gonna beg to give it back to him. But you haven't. Not yet, George."

"How can I give it back to him when I never took it?" asked Shepard.

"All right," said Goldy. "So Kirby stole it from the room before he kicked off. But you've got it now. Where is it?"

So there it was out in the open. He knew it was true but he said, "How do I know it was stolen? Kirby said he won it in a poker game. Sortino backed him up. If it was stolen, why didn't you go to the cops?''

"The cops?'' Goldy began to laugh mirthlessly.

"You prove to me that it was stolen,'' said Shepard, "and that Sortino got it legally in the first place, and I'll take you to where you can find it.''

"Let me beat his brains out a while,'' said the big one called Jake. "He'll soften up.''

"Listen, bastard,'' hissed Goldy, leaning closer, "how long you think we're gonna let you stall? The party's over, sonny. Wise up or you'll have a bad accident tonight. They'll be shoveling you up in the morning like so much crap on the road. You got thirty seconds, and all I wanna hear about is what you did with the cash.''

"And after I get it for you, then what?'' said Shepard. He already knew the answer. He wouldn't have to find out the hard way — like Rick Trainor.

"Then we give you a boot in the ass for being a wise guy and we let you go,'' said Goldy. He made it sound straight. But the one called Jake was smiling slyly. He was a dead giveaway.

Shepard shrugged. "Okay,'' he said. "I'm better off broke than dead.''

"Now you're using your bean, Georgie boy,'' said Goldy. "Where is it?''

"Under the seat,'' said Shepard. "In the back.'' Time was running out. In another minute they'd be taking him away.

Goldy gave Jake a look. "Thought I told you to take the inside apart. Get it!''

Jake got in and began to maneuver the seat, hoisting it out. "It's not here,'' he growled.

Goldy's face was breaking into angry pieces.

"Flip the seat over and look inside under the lining,'' said Shepard. He turned away from Goldy and looked into the back where Jake was scowling. As he had expected, Goldy followed his gaze, peering eagerly at Jake poking the lining, then ripping it open.

Shepard saw all this out of the corner of his eye, and when Jake's arm disappeared into the opening and there was the sound of spring coils complaining, he pivoted sharply in a swing so powerful that when his fist ground flesh against bone, Goldy toppled backward without a sound. Shepard didn't care what the rule book said about the vicious kick he placed in Goldy's groin before he touched earth — or the way he stomped on Goldy's windpipe while he plucked the .45 from limp fingers, all in a matter of seconds. His rules were U.S. Infantry, Korea, where he had told the men of his platoon: In hand-to-hand combat there is just this to remember: Only one of you is going to walk away — the fastest, the meanest, the dirtiest-fighting sonofabitch of the two. Be sure you're that man!

Bent over in the back seat of the car, the big bruiser called Jake had been at a disadvantage from the beginning. Shepard was counting on that. But not too much.

It must have taken Jake a startled moment to see that something had gone wrong, another moment or two to appraise the situation and a beat of time to overcome the inertia of adjustment and move. For he was just now bending out the door and advancing like a monstrous locomotive gathering steam.

Shepard was pulling upright over Goldy's last twitching, .45 in hand, when Jake came at him.

"Don't try it," he said. "This gun has no friends."

But Jake, who had not made a move for a weapon of his own, had the look of a machine set to kill. And the machine was going to grind on until its mechanism was silenced.

Shepard had the will of the Korean battlefield — but not the license. He couldn't kill this man. So he reversed the gun and, when Jake had all but engulfed him, jerked sideways and brought the butt down on the big man's skull. Even then, he had to hit him again before Jake sagged and went down.

He could find no weapon on Jake. Probably Jake thought he didn't need one. But he did find car keys — two sets. His own and the ones to the Buick. The latter he tested to be sure, then hurled across the road into the trees.

He swung the convertible around and waited with his motor idling. Goldy was the first to come out of it, crawling to his knees then spotting Jake and stumbling over. With a little help from Goldy, Jake was sitting up in about two minutes. His was a hard skull to damage.

Satisfied that he wasn't going to stand trial for homicide, even in self-defense, Shepard gave a last look to the café. Dimly he could see the hunched form of the paunchy man, eyes still glued to the television set, the young couple head-to-head at the other end of the bar and the blowzy barmaid reading a newspaper as she absently wiped a glass with what would be the same dirty towel. Nothing had changed. The whole affair had gone unnoticed.

Shepard couldn't help smiling as he gunned back onto the highway.

Chapter Fifteen

*T*here was an all-night drugstore a block east of Corinne's place on the Drive, and Shepard parked on a side street just beyond it. He was in a hurry. It was five minutes past one a.m., and the house detective, Mike Connors, should have finished his trick and might even be an his way home.

But, after placing the call, he had Connors on the phone in a matter of seconds.

"My relief was a little late or you might have missed me," said the security officer. "What's on your mind, Shepard? Did you have any luck at the lake?"

"I had some good luck and some bad luck," said Shepard evasively. "Something else on my mind right now. You remember I asked you if you heard anyone called by name in that room?"

"Uh-huh."

"And you said somebody called the guy whose picture I showed you by a name that sounded like Kroger but that wasn't quite it."

"Right."

"Okay. Now, think hard. Was it Trainor?"

"What was that again?"

"T — like in train. Train-or."

"That's it, boy. You've got it. Trainor. I only heard it once but it comes to me now. Trainor."

"My God! Do you remember reading anything in the paper about a man by that name?"

"Nope. I've been known to go two days without reading the paper at all. Besides, the name didn't stick with me, and unless it was an item about something that happened at this hotel I wouldn't have made the connection."

"Thanks anyway, Connors. That's all I need to know."

"I'm getting mighty damn curious," said Connors. "Don't you think you ought to tell me what it's all about?"

"I might just do that later today," said Shepard. "I might even need your help."

"Any time. Just give me a call."

"Thanks. See you then, Connors."

"So long."

Shepard decided not to move the convertible. Chances were the overnight porkers had taken all the spaces in front of the Westbridge Manor, and it was only around the corner. He got the suitcase from under the hood and began to walk. He had his own gun and the .45 ready in his pocket. But he wasn't worried because it would probably be hours before Sortino's battered scouts could report back. By that time, if he could convince them, the police would be waiting over on Sutton Place.

As he approached the corner of Riverside Drive, a cream-colored Chrysler cruised for a parking space, found one and backed in across the street. Shepard came abreast of it cautiously, keeping in shadow. But the space was close by a street light, and Shepard soon saw that the car contained a man and woman, who immediately went into a tight clinch. After they broke apart and the woman moved to her window to adjust her make-up in the light, her face was in profile and Shepard could see the sheen of long red hair.

It was Corinne.

The anger came upon Shepard slowly at first, as to one who knows a truth and still doesn't quite believe. Then he advanced on the car with the intention of going around to the driver's side, hauling the guy out, and beating him senseless.

But now it occurred to him that this would be about like hitting a man whose dog is biting you. So in disgust, he turned and began to walk away in the direction he had come.

Once he looked aback. The man was getting out and taking Corinne by the arm. He was a big powerful looking man.

The hell with her! If she needs a flunky, let him take care of her.

Shepard moved off down the street, put the suitcase under the hood, and reentered the drug store.

He sat at the counter drinking black coffee. Jealousy mounted in him and then left him as suddenly as it had come. He felt only a great, tired emptiness. He couldn't even hate her. It was worse than hate. It was like clear spring water emptying into a sewer — the slow draining away of the shining conceptions that had once made up The Dream.

There were things to be done. No matter how he felt, no matter how little heart he had for it now, someone had to clean up the debris before it caught fire and destroyed again. And he alone knew the truth. That was the trouble — he knew too much of truth, all the wrong kind.

Again he went to the phone, looked up a number, dialed.

Louise Buckley's sleepy voice answered.

"I'm sorry to wake you up, Louise. But it's important."

"Lonely Eyes?"

"I can't even laugh at that one. I've got to see you right away. I want you to take care of two hundred thousand dollars for me."

"No!"

"Yes. And be prepared for a worse shock. I know what happened to your boss."

"For heaven's sake, tell me!" She sounded wide-awake now.

"I'd rather not on the phone."

"I'll make coffee. Where are you?"

"Not far. I have a car and it won't take long at this hour."

"You have the address?"

"Got it from the phone book. Hold on, I'll be right over."

"You sound so upset. And tired."

"The year's understatement. 'Bye."

He hung up.

*L*ouise Buckley had the second-floor flat of a brownstone house located in the east seventies. The bay windows in the living room were edged with plaid, flounced curtains. The furniture was Early American, and the room was embellished with feminine frills and warm touches of color.

Louise was dressed in a gray skirt and powder-blue sweater. She looked wide-awake and, in spite of her haste, managed neatness and simple charm in her grooming. Her eyes were alert with curiosity and hardly-concealed worry.

Shepard set the red leather suitcase by a chair and sank into it wearily. Louise glanced at the case, frowned, and began serving coffee from an electric percolator.

"Since you found the money, I suppose I should be

serving champagne," she said with a wry smile. "But you don't seem overjoyed."

"That's because there's a lot of blood on this money and I don't think it's going to wash."

She looked startled.

He opened the case and watched her.

Her eyes widened. "I've never seen so much money at one time in my whole life."

"If you know the source, the thrill is gone," he said, closing the case and sliding it across the rug toward her. "Do me a favor and hide this in a safe place far a day or two. Then I might be ready to turn it over to the police."

"The police!"

He nodded.

"Why do you want me to keep it?"

"I think it once belonged to your boss. And obviously I can't carry it around with me. So, put it away and I'll explain."

She picked up the case dubiously and took it to another room. When she returned and sat waiting with a puzzled expression, he unfolded the story with a cold detachment, rushing along with it because he felt a vague uneasiness, a rising sense of urgency. In a flat voice he told of Corinne and the man in the Chrysler, finally recounting his phone conversation with Connors, making it clear that Trainor was in reality Martin Kroger.

She nodded and kept an nodding in a kind of stupor. "Then he's dead," she said.

"I'm sorry, Louise. And I hope there was nothing personal —"

She squeezed her eyes shut, as if blotting out an unbearable picture. "No. But I knew him well. At least I thought I did. And he — he was a human being, not some — some . . . ." Her voice trailed off. "How could they torture him like that? Oh, Neil, how could they!"

He got up and began to pace restlessly. "I don't know, I don't know, Louise. Why does anyone do anything? Why do I give a damn now about Corinne? I shouldn't. It doesn't make sense. But I do. Even after everything that's happened, I still do. It's like a disease with me."

She looked at him compassionately. "I wish I had the cure for that kind of disease."

"She's a spoiled bitch!" he said. "She's selfish to her toenails. Intellectually, I know it — and yet emotionally I cling to her or something she represents, like an alcoholic to his last bottle."

He stopped pacing just long enough to light a cigarette. He wanted to forget now. He wanted to be doing something. "Well," he said, "this kind of talk isn't getting anywhere." He sat down abruptly. "I've got to figure what to do next, and nothing brilliant comes to me at all. I'll probably have to exhaust the English language explaining to the police. Hell, the whole thing is such a tangle I can hardly understand it myself, let alone explain it."

"Now," Louise said, "what can I do to help?"

He looked at her. At that moment he had the feeling of complete unity with her. She had such a nice unaffected face. The eyes were clear, frankly penetrating, the mouth sensitive, kind. The features altered swiftly changing emotions, each expression so powerfully describing the feeling behind it that words were almost unnecessary. It was like watching the deeply moving play of thought on the face of a fine actress.

Suddenly a feeling of uneasiness stole over him. And he knew why. It occurred to him that if Goldy or the massive Jake phoned Sortino that he had escaped and they had failed to find the money, Sortino might get another idea. . . .

"Louise! Let me use your phone. I think I'd better call Corinne."

She smiled. "Incurable," she said. "I pronounce you incurable."

"No," he said. "It's something else."

"On the table by the window," she said, standing. "Shall I leave?"

He gave her a negative shake of the head, crossed to the phone, and dialed Corinne's number. As he listened to the metallic, dispassionate ringing, he watched Louise absently. She was sitting tensely on the arm of her chair, looking at him with the anxious air of one who roots for the underdog. The commiseration in her face made him wonder at her selflessness. Her boss was murdered, she was sick with shock and probably out of a job — and yet she could worry over his problems.

"Ten!" he said and. hung up.

"Ten what?"

"Ten rings and no circus," he said.

She laughed. "Well, you haven't lost your sense of humor. There's hope for you."

"I can't remember when I had a sense of humor," he said. "It might have been yesterday. But that was a long time ago."

"They may have stopped for a drink," she offered.

He shook his head. "No. They were on the way in. Either she's not answering or she's not there. Neither one sounds right. She was expecting to see me or hear from me about the money. In that case, she would be home waiting and alone. Or I don't know anything about her at all. Something's wrong."

"Maybe you'd better go up there and take the police with you."

He crossed to the door, turned. "The police? Oh, no. Not now. It would take a solid hour of explaining to get to first base with them."

She came and stood next to him by the door. "Let me know if there's anything at all I can do," she said. "And please be careful, Lonely Eyes."

"Why do you call me, that?" he said. "I don't mind. But I've never considered myself lonely."

"Oh, but you are," she said. "Awfully. I'm sorry if that sounds rude. It's just that I can t help worrying about you, Neil. You seem so mixed up, and I want to do something about it but I can't."

"I like you," he said. "I like you very much."

Impulsively he kissed her, clung to her. Her answering kiss was warm and strong.

He opened the door quickly and went out.

By the time he reached the convertible, in a frenzy of haste, he had forgotten her.

Chapter Sixteen

"Aw, now listen," said Lloyd Gannon at the door. "It's early yet. Why don't I come in and keep you company for a couple of hours?"

"No!" said Corinne. "I told you, no. Aren't you ever satisfied?"

Lloyd gave her his sly, insinuating grin. "Never," he said. "Not where you're concerned, hon. The hunger won't go away.''

"Go home and eat raw meat," she said. "I'm going to bed. And to sleep!"

"When will I see you?"

"Be busy for a few days," she said. "Give me a call the first of next week."

"Right." He kissed her, said, "So long, hon," and walked jauntily toward the elevator.

She watched the swing of his shoulder going away. A lot of man, she thought. My God, maybe too much.

When the elevator door closed, she began digging around in her purse for the key, finally locating it. Pushing it in the lock, she was wondering if Neil were waiting inside and if he had been watching the entrance from the window. If so, it didn't matter. She had a ready explanation. Her girl friend had a boyfriend. The boyfriend had dropped in unexpectedly and offered to drive her home. Corinne was so accustomed to needing an alibi that she always had one ready — just in case. Her lovers were usually jealous, and in the past this had saved her many a scene.

But looking up from below, she had observed that the apartment was dark. So it was likely that Neil was still on the road. She hoped he hadn't phoned.

She opened the door and went in, feeling for the light switch with one hand, bolting the door with the other. In those seconds before she found the switch, she became aware that there was a heavy smell of cigarette smoke in the room, like the stale aftermath of a party. It was odd, and she wondered if by any chance Neil had . . .

Her fingers found the switch, the light went on, and she turned.

A tortured sound burst from her throat.

There were three men seated in the living room facing her. Two sat like stone on the sofa, one in a chair, all of them smoking. Their faces were empty. One of the men on the sofa was gigantic. His features had a flat, beaten look, as though all emotion had been battered from them. He had a small bandage above his right temple. The other had curly blond hair and pink-rimmed serpent eyes in a face so bloodless the purple bruise on his cheekbone looked like the swelling symptom of some evil disease. The one in the chair had a face like a naked skull over which dark skin had been drawn so tightly that all the bones were visible. Except for the black, shiny marbles in the deep sockets, this face was the deadest of all.

Watching them, Corinne felt disembodied, as if stepping from reality into the somber threat of some silent and grotesque nightmare. The faces drifted and swayed as though seen through fathoms of water. Cigarette smoke eddied and rose toward the surface. Yet even in dark dreams there is the instinct of preservation and the hand in back of her groped upward along the door paneling for the bolt she should never have closed, locking her on the wrong side of safety.

"Come away from that door, Red."

It was the one with the bruised face and the red-rimmed eyes who had spoken. Hearing the voice made it all suddenly real and more frightening in a different way.

"Who — who are you?" she whispered.

"Come and see, little girl," said the skull-faced one . . . "Come and see."

"No," she said. "No, I won't" She felt as if something had left her. The thing that made her proud and tall and in command of her world had fled from her, leaving as small, frail shell. "I don't know you," she said. "What do you want with me?"

"Come here and stand in front of my chair," ordered the skull-faced one. "And be quick about it!"

Mentally she had turned and was frantically opening, the door, running down the hall screaming for
help. . . . Actually she was moving toward the man, putting one hesitant foot down after the other. There was
something as undeniable as death in his eyes.

"That's better," he was saying now as she paused
in, front of him: "Much better."

"Jesus, God!" said the gigantic one, leaning forward
from the sofa. "What a looker, huh, Vic?"

"Shut up!" said the skull-faced one called Vic. And
then to her — "Your name is Corinne Kirby. Correct?"

"Yes," she said. "Please tell me what you want.
Please!" They knew her name, then. And there was no
mistake.

"The man who was with you — his name and his
business," said the one called Vic.

"He — why should I tell you anything?"

The black eyes simply looked at her.

"His name is Lloyd Gannon," she said. "He's sales
manager for a tire company."

"He went away, Goldy?" sand Vic to the blond man.

"Yeah. I signaled Max to lay off of him."

Vic nodded. "Well now, tell me, Corinne, where is
the boyfriend — Shepard?"

"I don't know."

"You don't know?" The dark, eyebrows arched
slightly.

"No. He said he would phone."

"Never mind. We'll get him. Now — where did you
and the boyfriend hide the money?"

She was beginning to understand now, and it was
worse than she had thought. She opened her purse. "I
have about thirty dollars."

"Thirty dollars," said Goldy, the blond one. "Did
you hear that, Vic? Thirty bucks."

"I heard," said Vic. "Listen, little girl. Don't play

hide-and-seek with me. I want the two hundred thousand Kirby stole from the hotel room.''

So that's where he'd gotten it. "I don't know what you're talking about," she said.

He didn't even get up. His hard, bony hand reached out and grabbed her wrist, pulling her down to her knees. The other hand opened and smashed across her face. The pain brought tears to her eyes.

"Don't lie to me, little girl. Don't ever lie to me. Where's the dough?"

"Dough?" How silly. How useless to stall.

"She don't speak our language," said the big one.

"She's gonna learn words she never heard of before the night's over," said Goldy.

"Once more," said the one called Vic. "Just once more. Where did you hide the money — the two hundred thousand dollars?"

"My husband hid it in the basement."

"Ahhh. Well then, suppose we go down and get it."

"But after he hid it," she said from her kneeling position, "he moved it again and now I don't know where it is. He died without telling."

The hand struck her brutally on the other side of the face, and she began to sob.

"Listen, little girl. One man has died very slowly already, screaming he didn't know. You think because you're a woman and beautiful it will go any easier with you? For a woman it's very hard. There are such soft, such tender places. Don't be foolish. It's better for you to talk *now*." He released her.

Corinne stood up, wiping her eyes. She looked at each in turn. The eyes of the blond one were obscene with lust. The big one leered hungrily. The other was only an empty skull with cold, empty eyes. There was no hope of sympathy.

"I'll tell you everything I know," she said. Truthfully, desperately, she unfolded the entire story.

"This Sortino you mention," said the one called Vic, "You know who that is? *I* am Victor Sortino."

"You," she whispered.

"Yes," said Sortino. "So obviously, if I ever knew this Kirby, he would have died sooner. The story is a fake out of your stupid brain."

"I can't help it," she pleaded. "I only know what my husband told me — that he won the money gambling."

"I don't care what he told you," said Sortino. "Where is the money now?"

"Why won't you listen to me? I don't know! My friend is out looking for it."

"Her friend is out looking for it," mimicked Goldy. "Bastard damn near ruined me. I'm gonna kill that sonofabitch."

"Wise guy beats me over the head and takes the keys," said the giant one. "If it wasn't we jumped the switch we'd still be coolin' our tails. Jesus — we come back here like a goddamn rocket, doin' eighty-ninety all the way. But we never found the sonofabitch."

"Might be he came a different road," said Goldy. "Or he was goin' someplace else."

"All right — cut it!" snapped Sortino. "Don't give me excuses. You loused it up. Lucky Max and I covered here or we wouldn't even have this little fish to fry." He turned to Corinne. "You heard them," he said. "They followed your boyfriend up to some lake. He went around a bend in the road and turned off somewhere. They lost him and picked him up again on the way back. He didn't have the two hundred grand with him. So now I'm going to tell you what really happened. He had it with him but he had it on the way up. He wasn't looking for it at all. When he got there, he hid it some place. And you're going to tell us exactly where that place is."

"I can't tell you," she said, "because I don't know."

"You don't know," said Sortino, sarcastically. "You don't know. This lover-boy is sleeping around with you, laying toesies in your bed, he was in with you from the beginning — and you don't know."

"No," she said. "I don't know, he doesn't know. My husband was the only one who ever knew, and he's dead. I think he took the money to some place in Connecticut. I don't know where. We were trying to find out."

Sortino nodded. "I thought that would be your story. You haughty, lying bitch! You think you don't stink like the rest of us? You think you won't scream and beg? You think you won't bleed and die? Where is that two hundred grand!"

"I don't know. Please! I don't, I don't!" She was so terribly frightened, and she could feel her clothes sweatstuck to her body.

"Jake," said Sortino to the big one. "You want to beat some sense into her?"

Jake came to tower over her. Corinne could smell the stale acrid stench of body odor. "Now," he said. "Now, Vic. I don't wanna beat this one. I wanna love 'er to death."

"What a way to go," said Goldy. "Bet I could have the truth right out of her."

"Jake," said Sortino, "how long since you had a woman?"

Jake laughed, a kind of nervous giggle. "'Bout a month now," he said. "Jesus! I got to have this one." His big paw reached up and grabbed her breast, squeezed brutally. She shrank back but the other hand had clamped over her buttocks, holding her fast. The smell and fear of him made her sick.

"Goldy," said Sortino. "Would you like some of this, too?"

"So help me," said Goldy. "I'd give a grand for it."

"But two hundred grand is another thing, eh?"

"For that you could buy a thousand much more willing," said Goldy.

"I don't like 'em willing," said Jake, still maintaining his hold.

Sortino fastened Corinne with his black, empty stare. "These boys are not like your silk-handkerchief lovers, eh? They don't ask politely. They don't touch gently." His voice rose. "They rip and tear! You want me to turn you over to them?"

"No! Please!"

"Then where is the dough!"

"Get your dirty hands off me," she said to Jake.

"Let her go," said Sortino.

Jake stepped away, drooling.

"The two hundred grand," said Sortino. "Where is it?"

"Look," she said. "I'm not very brave. I'm not brave at all. If I knew I wouldn't dare not tell you. But I don't know. I wouldn't know where to begin to look. Can't you see I'm scared out of my mind? If my husband stole your money, then you should have it back. I don't want it. I don't want any part of it. But for the last time, I don't know where it is."

They passed looks around the room to each other.

"This one has more shape than brains," said Sortino. "She's going to be a problem to us. I can see that. A big headache. We're going to have to put the screws to her."

"Yeah," said Goldy. "Yeah."

"We'll have to maul her," said Sortino. "Before she'll talk, we'll have to worry her to death."

"Not here," said Jake. "These walls won't hold them screams."

"No," said Sortino. "Not here. Goldy, while we wrap her mouth, you go down and check if it's clear. Tell Max we'll flash him when we're ready. If it's okay, have him give us two winks with the headlights. Three if we should hold off.''

"Right," said Goldy. He departed.

"Okay, Jake," said Sortino. "Just the hands behind the back. And then the mouth.''

As Jake was tying her hands, she sucked in her breath for the scream. Then, thinking better of it, she exhaled. They were bloodless, brutal. They might kill her on the spot. Better to wait and hope.

They were getting ready to gag her when Goldy came back.

"Well?" said Sortino.

"It's clear now," answered Goldy.

"All right," said Sortino. "But when we go down, you get the shotgun out of the trunk and ride that rear window.''

"Got you," said Goldy.

"Now the gag," said Sortino to Jake.

"Wait!" said Corinne. "I have something to say."

"She's wising up," said Jake.

"Well?" said Sortino. "Speak. And hurry it up."

Corinne looked at each of them and then pulled her ace. "If you take me one step out of this apartment," she said, "that's kidnapping. Do you know what the penalty is for kidnapping? The electric chair.''

Sortino nodded and Jake gave her a short jab in the Adam's apple with the edge of his hand. Her mouth flew open, and Jake quickly jammed the breach with the gag and tied it securely.

"What's the penalty for murder, Goldy?" said Sortino.

Goldy grinned. "The chair," he said. "The old juice to the butt!''

"Then let's go," said Sortino. "What have we got to lose?''

Chapter Seventeen

Shepard stood outside the door to Corinne's apartment and looked at his watch. It was twenty minutes after two a.m. He took the key Corinne had given him from his pocket. For a moment he stood with his ear to the door, listening, he removed Goldy's Colt .45 from his pocket, liking the heavy, solid feel of a weapon he understood, whose remorseless striking power he had seen in war. He checked the automatic to see that there was a round in the chamber before cocking it. Doing all this he felt a little foolish. These precautions were probably unnecessary.

Silently he opened the door, just enough to admit his hand. He groped for the wall switch, found it. Light fell from the overhead fixture. He gave the door a kick.

The living room was deserted. The heavy odor of tobacco, recently smoked, clung to the room. Probably the man had come in with Corinne, remained a while, and left. On the other hand, maybe —

Shepard flipped switches, lighting his way around the rest of the apartment. Corinne's bedroom was a mess. Drawers were open, clothing was spilled about the room. Shoes, dresses, hatboxes spilled from a closet. The mattress was overturned.

In the kitchen he found more disarray. Even the oven door stood open. His heart sank. A horror of anxiety stole over him.

Back in the living room, below the pillowed sofa, he found a cigarette butt that had been ground into the rug. He picked it up, studying the frayed, blackened end. There was a small burn on the carpet. It had been an act of pure contempt. He found several more butts in ashtrays — too many butts in too many trays.

Shepard was in a fever of tormenting worry and indecision. The police? They did not jump into squad cars and fly into action at an alarm sounded by some possible crackpot who claimed his girl *might* have been kidnapped. They sat and listened and nodded politely, and they took notes and filled out reports and asked interminable questions. Then they began a careful but unburned investigation, making sure not to trample the rights of private citizens on the strength of a singe unfounded accusation.

No, in his haste, Shepard was still and, it seemed, always alone.

*H*e kept jabbing and jabbing the doorbell and frantically hammering with his fist. She came at last in a pink nightgown, which she attempted to conceal by drawing the robe tighter around her. She looked pale and frightened.

"Louise!" he said. "For God's sake, don't ask questions. Get the key you told me you have to Kroger's apartment. Bring it to me. Run!"

Her mouth fell open and clamped shut. Her eyes surveyed him with pity. She went for the key without a word, gave it to him. "Try to keep your head," she said. "Don't do anything foolish."

"Get dressed," he said. "Go to the police — in person. It may carry more weight. Tell them the facts quickly. Most important — tell them that Corinne Kir-by's apartment has been ransacked and that she's been kidnapped. Just because she's a woman,'' he choked, "they won't treat her any better than Kroger. See if you can persuade them to send a squad car to meet me at Kroger's — Sortino's apartment.

"And, Louise, take a taxi and go with the money. Two hundred thousand dollars might be a better argument than anything you could say.''

"I'll go this minute,'' she said. "Oh, my God, Neil, I'm sorry. I'm so sorry.''

"Do what you can, Louise. Good-bye.''

He raced down and across town to Sutton Place, parking the car in the shadows where it would not serve as a warning.

"You know Mr. Sortino?'' he said to the elevator boy.

"Yes, sir.''

"Has he come in yet?''

"No, sir. Not since midnight when I came on.''

"Anyone else go to his apartment?''

"No, sir. Not that I know of. Only one stop at fourteen — Mr. and Mrs. Coleman.''

"All right,'' he said. "My name is Shepard, and I'm going up there. If Mr. Sortino comes in, you're not to mention that I'm waiting. If you do, you'll lose your job. This is police business. Understand?''

"Yes, sir,'' the elevator boy said meekly, obviously wishing he understood more.

"Now if some uniformed policemen or plain-clothes men arrive, tell them I'm up there. But if they're not in uniform, make sure you know who you're talking to first.''

"Very well, sir, I'll make sure. Do you mind if I ask — ?''

"Yes, I do mind. Now, take me to fourteen.''

After the elevator had gone below, he again found himself standing before a locked door with a drawn gun, opening the door cautiously. This time he didn't find the switch so easily. He had to step in to reach it. He needn't have worried — in a minute he had darted from room to room and found the apartment empty. Nor could he find a shred of paper or other clue that told him anything he had to know. And they were not so stupid as to bring her here . . .

On an off chance, he located the phone and dialed Corinne's number. It rang and rang into frightful emptiness.

Now he sat in darkness facing the char, the .45 on his lap. He sat so still and listened so attentively it was almost painful. Occasionally he thought he detected the hum of the elevator and the clatter of its door. It was a distant sound. The car might be stopping just below or above — never at fourteen.

Once he heard the muted peak and fall of a siren. The sound grew upon the night, then faded and diminished altogether with his hope. In Christ's name, where were they? And what could they do if they came?

From time to time he hovered at the window, but he could see only the empty street with its shadowy lights and the black trail of the river.

The immobility of it — the waste of time crushing onward. Ten minutes until four a.m. Somewhere in a side-street police station there were empty corridors and plain rooms with scarred desks — The musty smell of ancient wood and the bleak, cold feel of quiet deliberation and timeless enforcement. Somewhere in one of the too bright, too sad rooms of such a station was the frail Louise with the earnest eyes and the suitcase containing two hundred thousand dollars. Louise explaining and pleading. And the white face of the officer with the grave eyes nodding and not being in the least astonished —

except perhaps at the sight of more money than he could earn after taxes in forty years of service. And his saying, "Now let me get his straight, madam. You state that you think — you don't know for sure — that your boss, a Martin Kroger, has been murdered. And this money belonged to him. And now this Mrs. what's-her-name — Kirby — whose husband stole the money, may have been kidnapped. But you're not certain of that, either. You must admit, madam, it's a little confusing. We can't very well act without some verification. Now again — who is this man you want us to arrest? What is his business and exactly what crime can you prove that he has committed?"

And while it is not the officer's fault that he must move with caution, a hundred squad cars could be summoned from a dozen precincts were he to lift the phone at his elbow and make the appropriate sounds.

And while he questioned, there were questions being asked in a much more secret and private room of that city. And when the answers were not forthcoming, the treatment was not so gentle though the flesh was dust as tender. . . .

In a half hour of silence Shepard's nerves were exploding with the need of action. He couldn't stay there in the gutted darkness. He couldn't wait. He had to move somewhere. So he made a last, useless call to Corinne's apartment and went back down to the street. If the police came, he would be there to meet them. If Sortino came, he would be watching.

He pulled the convertible closer and waited, wrenching at the wheel as though he could tear it away to release his excess of steam.

At thirty-two minutes after four o'clock by his watch, the dark Buick pulled up before 80 Sutton Place South. Sortino and a slim, dapper man whom Shepard had never seen before alighted. They moved into the building with the quick step of men who are in haste to perform some mission.

Shepard squirmed, clenched his hands, and controlled the urge to follow. He had the distinct feeling that they would not remain above long. The Buick had been parked too carelessly, and there was the insinuation of a tense and brief errand. So Shepard swung the convertible to a position not far behind the Buick.

He was right in waiting. In ten minutes, the pair returned to the street. Each was carrying a heavy suitcase which they tossed in the back of the car. Then they sped off, with Shepard in careful pursuit.

He did not like the look of those suitcases. Sortino was on the run. With the two hundred thousand still unfound, it could mean something too ugly for Shepard to allow himself a moment of speculation. He could only follow. This, at least, was action.

Traffic was light, but enough cars interposed for concealment. The Buick wheeled west on 57th Street, then turned uptown on West End Avenue. Traffic was even thinner here, so Shepard took a chance and blacked out his lights just before rounding the corner. He could see well enough, if some cruising squad car didn't nab him. That would be ironic — he could be arrested for traveling without lights while murderers and kidnappers got away. And it was just the sort of thing to happen.

But it didn't. Sortino's Buick proceeded uptown for some distance, then swung right into a side street. Two blocks east it slowed and came to a halt. The taillights winked out.

Shepard had barely turned the comer, pulling to the curb to wait and watch. Now he also moved forward to within a block of the two cars, parked, and cut the motor. On foot, he crept forward over the lonely sidewalk.

The building was a dark, shabby, corner grocery store. Silently, Shepard tried the door but found it locked. There was an iron railing on either side of the store and, inside one of the railings, stone steps led below. Shepard brought out the .45 and moved down the steps to a slightly open door. He passed inside and felt his way along a dank corridor to a heavy, wooden door. Beneath this door there was a thin slash of light.

At first Shepard could hear nothing. But then, by pressing his ear against the door and straining, he picked up snatches of conversation — enough to freeze his heart forever.

First, the deep, mournful timbre of Sortino's voice — ". . . not with me, you're not. Goddamn blundering ape. . . ! Going nowhere with us. Just beat it. Get lost, Jake."

". . . too hard maybe, but I didn't mean to bump her, Vic — honest!"

". . . and your goddamn big fist. . . ! might have talked and then you screwed it for good . . . killed her . . . can't risk it now . . . leave town."

Shepard slumped, gasping, was sick and wanted to throw up. The voices droned and he didn't hear them. He stood there for a void of time, still trying to grasp a feeble hope that he had misunderstood. He built an icy bulwark against the emotion inside him. It was temporary but it gave him the needed clarity.

Slowly he tried the knob and pushed gently. He was not much surprised when the door gave a fraction. They had been careless under the pressure of fear and haste.

He could see them now. Four men in a basement room under the naked glare of an overhead light. They were grouped around the foot of an iron bed — Sortino, Goldy, Jake, and the nameless one, darkly dapper and thin.

They looked down. Shepard could not see what lay on the bed. They were grouped too tightly around it. But over the side he could see a long, slender arm, with its

lifeless, manicured fingers. He knew it was Corinne —
and that she was dead.

"Jesus, what a waste!" Goldy was saying. "Even
now, if you can take your eyes off that face, she's some
looker. Christ, but that face makes me sick. And I've got
a strong gut."

"We can't leave her here," said Sortino. His features were without a trace of emotion. He simply looked
at her as though at some inanimate puzzle. "They'll
trace her to Jake, and maybe Jake to us. Cover her up.
We'll take her along in the trunk, and I'll think of something on the way."

"Why don't we stake out the boyfriend first?" said
Goldy. "That Shepard bastard."

"Why don't you do that?" said Shepard from the
doorway. "But now, turn around with eight hands showing and all empty!"

There was a moment of solid immobility. Then
Goldy threw a glance over his shoulder and came around
with his hands up. The thin, dapper one followed suit.
Sortino didn't turn at all. And Jake swung fast with a
sawed-off shotgun that could only have been lying at the
foot of the bed.

It went off do an angry blast at the ceiling — a reflex
action. Jake was already dead from the .45 caliber slug
Shepard had sent through his brain.

At almost the same instant, Sortino whirled, a fountain pen appearing in his hand. The move didn't make
sense to Shepard until it went off and a bullet scraped
the side of his neck with no more sensation than the sting
of a bee.

If there was an expression on Sortino's face, it was
one of disappointment and it vanished quickly. In the
next moment a slug tore through his windpipe, he fell.
And now Shepard could see the bed.

Corinne's ayes were open and sightless in the

ghastly way of brutal death. Her swollen features were broken and dried blood ran in a thin stream from her shattered nose. She was naked.

Goldy was cringing back against the bed, hands high. The thin, dapper one looked down at the draining bodies of Jake and Sortino and trembled — he couldn't stop trembling. Then he trite to speak and couldn't.

"You animals!" Shepard snarled. "You loathsome, crawling, stinking animals. How could you!"

"No!" said Goldy. "No! We didn't know he was gonna kill her. We had nothing to do with it."

Shepard advanced, put the gun in his pocket. He was a giant. Ten men couldn't kill him. He struck Goldy first — so hard that he went over the rail of the bed and toppled off to the floor. The dapper one ran, but Shepard caught him at the door and slowly, methodically beat him unconscious.

It was over. . . .

Shepard went to the bed now and touched her brow timidly. He shuddered and began to weep. Sobbing, he covered her naked body with the soiled spread and carried her to the corridor where he laid her down gently. He wasn't going to leave her in that room.

He went back and, searching pockets for weapons, found the door key on big Jake's slimy remains. He looked around the room. It was windowless, and there was no other exit. There was a small ax and an assortment of tools on a bench. He gathered these with the shotgun and lethal pen and dumped them outside. He returned, and again he searched for any implement that could open a door so strong half a dozen men could not shoulder it down, let alone two. There was nothing. But when he found a coil of rope in a drawer, he tied the unconscious men anyway. Then he went out, locking the door and testing it, leaving the key in the lock. He did all this with a numb coolness.

The corridor was dark, so he flared his lighter and took a last look at Corinne. Then he covered her face with the spread and stumbled out to the street.

There was a mild surprise in him that the sound of the shots had not reached out to awaken the neighborhood and bring the police. But the shabby buildings had vacant eyes and their tenants continued in dumb slumber. The street was barren of traffic or sound.

He began to walk. Though he could hear the hushed, early-morning voices of the city echoing from its canyon streets and dark-faced rivers, he felt a sense of unreality. There was no space or time, he was without physical sensation. The movement of his limbs, the slight far of his steps on the pavement were unfelt. The yellow Cadillac was forgotten, and now even the dreadful picture of that basement room had faded. He was nothing.

He walked a mile of blocks without awareness, and then a subtle change crept over him. He was again able to think with some clarity around the throbbing wound of despair in his chest.

The police. Should he call the police? He listened to himself, reporting — there has been a murder, a woman in the basement of a grocery store. Woman? Would he use the word — woman? Such a cold, dead sound. Who is this woman? I — I don't know. . . . Well yes, I know, officer. But I — I can't say her name. . . . Why? Because then, you see, it would be true. . . . Crazy? Yes. Yes, officer, I guess I am. And then the line would go silent as the officer dismissed it — just another crank.

But he would call. Yes, he would call. And he would find something to say, though he was not yet able to answer in person their dispassionate questions, telling him not to get excited, not to get upset or muddled — just give them the facts. Anyway, did it matter? Now? Would a few hours or even a day — make any difference?

No, he did not want to talk with the police in person

He was like the man who, at his hanging, when asked if he had anything to say, replied, "No. Not at this time." But he did want to talk with someone. Talk around this thing, until with a single word — dead — he could touch the center.

But in all the city, in all the world, he could think of no one with whom he could share such emptiness. Who could he tell of the night on the Astor Roof, so long ago, the music wailing of endless love — she, tall and proud in his arms, pressing too close against his thighs though her smile was demure? Who could listen and understand?

The answer came to him at the precise moment that he saw just ahead, set against the bleak darkness like a small, blazing ship in the night, the garish lights of an all-night diner.

He swung back the door of the beanery and entered. In spite of the hour, more than half the stools were taken. Workmen in the crude costumes of the day lifted coffee cups and talked in strident voices of commonplace things that, for Shepard, belonged to a world that was gone.

The air in the diner was old. The smothering food smells made Shepard think of decay, and he was sickened. He did not want a living soul to look into his face at that moment, and he shrank toward the public phone that was bracketed against the tile wall. But he need not have worried. This was New York, and no one paid him the slightest attention.

His back shielding him from the counter with its customers, he thumbed through the directory and found the nearest police precinct. He dropped the dime in the slot and dialed. When the voice answered, he asked for someone in homicide. A man who identified himself as Detective Sergeant Munnelly came on the line.

Shepard spoke softly but clearly. "My name is

Shepard, Munnelly," he said. "Neil Shepard."

"Shepard yes, sir."

"I want to report the murder of a — a young woman by four hoodlums, the leader called Victor Sortino. S-o-r-t-i-n-o. I caught the filthy animals and killed two of them in self-defense. The other two are tied and locked in a room. The key is in the lock. Have you got that?"

"Sure — I've got it. But now wait a minute, fella, I —"

"You'll want to know how to get there," said Shepard. "So take it down."

"Hold it, buddy, hold it! You'd better come in here and —"

"Take it down," Shepard said. "For God's sake, just take it down!" He felt himself breaking at the sound of a human voice. But he controlled himself. Sergeant Munnelly kept silent and took the information.

"That's it, Munnelly," Shepard said. "That's all."

"That's all! Listen, Shepard, you'd better —"

"I know your name and precinct," Shepard said. "When I get ready, I'll be in with the full story."

He hung up.

Again he dropped a coin and dialed.

"Hello, hello!" The voice was wide-awake.

"Louise?"

"Neil!"

For a moment, he wasn't able to speak.

"Lonely Eyes?" Her voice was softer.

If only she hadn't said that, he might have made it. He felt himself breaking again. He couldn't utter a word. But he did.

"Yes," he said, "that's right. Lone — Lonely Eyes."

He made a small, sobbing sound.

"Neil! Listen, dear, I tried. I did try! I took the money and I got the police to go over there. But you weren't —"

"I know, I know. It was too late anyway."

"Trouble? Bad trouble?"

"Yes. Bad trouble. Oh, God, Louise. Such bad trouble."

"Don't try to say any more. Now listen, you come right over. I'll be waiting. Where are you?"

"I — I don't know. I don't know where I am. Help me, Louise. Help me! I'm lost."

"Yes," she said. "I knew you were lost." Her voice was tender. "And I'll try to help you find yourself. But you'll have to find *me* first. Can you do that?"

"Yes. I'll take a taxi," he said, feeling calmer now. "About twenty minutes."

"Hold on, then," she said. "I'll be waiting. Just hold on."

"Goodbye, Louise," he said.

For a moment Shepard looked dumbly at the receiver in his hand.

Then he hung up.